# DANGEROUS HEIGHTS

Standing next to Morgan Newman on the balcony of his luxury high-rise apartment, Barbara looked down at glittering nighttime Chicago and felt for one intoxicating moment that she possessed the entire vast and throbbing city.

Then the scene below was forgotten as Morgan's lips met hers, as his arms pressed her against him. She felt her own arms go around his neck, almost under their own volition, and deep within her, in a place never touched before, a new longing was born.

"Maybe you shouldn't have come here tonight, Barbara," Morgan said softly.

"Why?"

"Because you're too beautiful to resist." And he brushed his fingertips over the white slope of Barbara's uncovered shoulder . . . a touch that demanded more . . . much more. . . .

ELEANOR FROST lives in Ohio, where she is the society editor of a small-town daily newspaper. She began her career in journalism as the staff photographer for a service newspaper at the Naval Air Station, Pensacola, Florida. She enjoys reading, sewing, and, of course, writing. She is the author of another Rapture Romance, *Elusive Paradise*.

Dear Reader:

We at Rapture Romance hope you will continue to enjoy our four books each month as much as we enjoy bringing them to you. Our commitment remains strong to giving you only the best, by well-known favorite authors and exciting new writers.

We've used the comments and opinions we've heard from *you*, the reader, to make our selections, so please keep writing to us. Your letters have already helped us bring you better books—the kind you want—and we appreciate and depend on them. Of course, we are always happy to forward mail to our authors—writers need to hear from their fans!

And don't miss any of the inside story on Rapture. To tell you about upcoming books, introduce you to the authors, and give you a behind-the-scenes look at romance publishing, we've started a *free* newsletter, *The Rapture Reader*. Just write to the address below, and we will be happy to send you each issue.

Happy reading!

The Editors
Rapture Romance
New American Library
1633 Broadway
New York, NY 10019

# A PUBLIC AFFAIR

*by*
**Eleanor Frost**

RAPTURE ROMANCE
NEW AMERICAN LIBRARY

### PUBLISHER'S NOTE

This novel is a work of fiction. Names, characters, places, and incidents either are the product of the author's imagination or are used fictitiously, and any resemblance to actual persons, living or dead, events, or locales is entirely coincidental.

SIGNET, SIGNET CLASSIC, MENTOR, PLUME, MERIDIAN and NAL BOOKS
are published by New American Library,
1633 Broadway, New York, New York 10019

First Printing, May, 1984

1 2 3 4 5 6 7 8 9

PRINTED IN THE UNITED STATES OF AMERICA

# Chapter One

❦

A group of children was playing stickball in the street, and Barbara had to stop short to avoid tripping over an eight-year-old who zipped onto the sidewalk to capture the ball. The child let out a cry of triumph as he scooped it up and executed an excellent broken-field maneuver; reversing his direction as quickly as he had run into her path, he made a deft detour around a parking meter and scored a goal by touching the ball to the third step of the entry to the adjacent apartment building. The young street athlete's teammates joined in to celebrate the play, and Barbara found herself cheering with them.

"Way to be, Babe!" she laughed.

"Who Babe?" the boy replied suspiciously as he regarded Barbara with dark, sparkling eyes. The children stopped to turn their attention to the intruding adult.

"Babe Ruth," Barbara replied. "The baseball player." The boy's blank expression told her that she was speaking to someone too young to know whom she was talking about. "Never mind," Barbara laughed, starting to walk again.

"Hey, lady!" the boy said, dropping into step beside her. "You got a boyfriend?" His dark face gleamed with mischief as he smiled his best con-man smile at her. Barbara stopped and smiled back at the boy.

"Not at the moment. But I'm afraid I'm in the market for someone a little taller. What's your name?"

"Ossie. If you gonna walk 'round here you gotta have a man to walk with you."

"Oh. I suppose you're offering your services?"

"Bad stuff could happen to a pretty redhead lady 'round here," he said gravely. The group of children, a mixture of black, Latino and white, had gathered nearby to watch Ossie hustle the white lady. Barbara registered some amusement as she watched them giggling and nudging each other.

"And what would you expect in return for these protective services?"

"You got a buck, lady?"

"Well, let me see," Barbara said seriously, bending down to come face to face with Ossie. "I don't think I could spare a dollar for a bodyguard, but maybe we could negotiate." Digging in her purse, she found the candy bar she had bought at noon and forgotten to eat. "How about if I give you this candy bar and you stay here to guard my retreat?"

Ossie looked unsure of himself. "Granny say I shouldn't take candy from strangers," he replied. A twitter of giggles rose from the watching crowd, and Barbara suppressed her own laugh. Ossie wasn't above hustling a buck, but he had scruples about taking candy from strangers.

"Your Granny is absolutely right," she said seriously.

"I really shouldn't have offered it. Do you like to dance, Ossie?"

"You gonna take me out for a night on the town?" the boy asked slyly. There was another chorus of giggles from their audience.

"No, but if you like to dance or act or anything like that, you can come to the place where I work tomorrow morning. I've got a friend there who gives lessons—even for fellows your size."

"What place is that?"

"The Thirty-seventh Street Center for the Performing Arts," she explained. "I know that's a mouthful, but everybody just calls it the Center. It's two blocks down, next to the drugstore. And because you're such a brave bodyguard, if you and all your friends drop by tomorrow, I'll find room for you in one of the classes."

"No jive?"

"Absolutely not. Just ask for Barbara Danbury." Barbara smiled and started to walk away as the children milled around and picked up their game again. With any luck, one or two of the children would show up at the Center. The drama and dance classes for young people were filling up slowly and every direct contact Barbara could make was a step in the right direction.

The Center was Barbara's pet project. A youth center for the performing arts in a decaying Chicago neighborhood was not the kind of charitable project that the conservative Calvin Foundation usually sponsored. The New York-based foundation was more likely to donate money to build an opera house in a city center, or fund a scholarship to an Ivy League school. But Barbara had used every bit of influence she had as a member of the board to get the Thirty-seventh Street Center in Chicago off the ground, and had even moved to the Windy City to help oversee and assure the Center's development.

She had rented an apartment in the neighborhood, hoping to get closer to the people she was trying to help. "And now I'm even recruiting on the streets," she chuckled to herself.

This was definitely not the kind of neighborhood she had grown up in. In fact, she couldn't honestly say she had grown up in any kind of a neighborhood. As Horace Calvin's ward, her childhood home had been a Manhattan penthouse. She vaguely remembered a house in New Jersey before she went to live with "Uncle" Horace, but those memories were so sketchy that they seemed to belong to someone else.

There had always been babysitters—Barbara's mother had died when she was an infant, and her father, Horace Calvin's personal attorney, was much too busy to take an active part in the rearing of his daughter. When Barbara was seven, her father died suddenly from a stroke. She had no close relatives and Barbara would have become a ward of the state, but Horace Calvin stepped in and agreed to become her guardian.

After she went to live with Uncle Horace, Barbara had received her education at private boarding schools, spent her summers traveling in Europe and never, ever had she played stickball in the city streets. Though she considered herself city-bred, Barbara had to admit that the urban decay of this Chicago neighborhood was a completely different world from the one she was accustomed to.

The neighborhood chosen for the Center was one of those in transition, home to a bewildering mixture of people. The older, retired, blue-collar population was giving way to a younger, racially-mixed group. Unemployment ran high in this area of the city, but there was still a solid core of families in the neighborhood. That was why the Center belonged here, it was a section that could be saved, with the right kind of help. The Center was planned as a place where previously unsupervised young people could get adult attention and help in developing their talents. At best, Barbara hoped that the Center's influence would be felt by a drop in neighborhood vandalism. At the very least, the Center would offer an opportunity to some performer of the future.

As the early summer evening light waned, Barbara quickened her step. It was still three blocks to her apartment building. She had no fear of the city streets, though she had enough sense to want to be home before it was completely dark. But she enjoyed this walk home from the Center each night; it gave her an opportunity to drink in the flavor of the neighborhood. Young couples sat out on the stoops, holding hands and listening to radios while younger children darted back and forth across the sidewalk. The odors of cooking in individual apartments overlayed the smell of exhaust fumes and the subtle hint of an occasional flower box or a potted shrub. Country people always complained about the smell of city air, but Barbara knew that it took a real born-and-bred city person to appreciate it. It was full of life. And you could appreciate the perfume of a flower much more when it was an unexpected reward.

A light breeze ruffled Barbara's short red curls. The demands of her new assignment precluded regular visits to the hairdresser, so she had gotten it cut in a style that required a minimum of trouble. Since coming to live and work in this neighborhood, she had also adopted a more casual way of dressing. Barbara had always enjoyed wearing the best in clothing, though she was far from wealthy. Horace Calvin left his millions to the Calvin Foundation, not his ward, but she had a comfortable salary from her position with the foundation, and one of her priorities had always been an attractive wardrobe. For her work in this neighborhood, however, her usual tailored suits and designer dresses would have been too conspicuous. With that in mind, she dressed neatly but unexceptionally, today in gray gabardine slacks and an apricot cotton blouse.

Not that the image she presented was plain. Barbara was tall, nearly five feet eleven, and she carried her height proudly, even daring to wear high heels. The dark-red shade of her hair brought out the warm tones of her complexion and light brown eyes. She moved with a confident grace, the legacy of a lifetime among confident, powerful people. At thirty she had a mature, self-possessed air that tended to make people take her seriously. Even the seven conservative financial experts who comprised the remainder of the Calvin Foundation board of directors were beginning to take her seriously, though it hadn't always been that way.

Horace Calvin's will had specified that Barbara would have a place on the board of the foundation. It was his way of providing for her. Horace had been a self-made man who believed that hard work was the way to success. When Barbara was a teenager, Horace had explained to her that while he didn't want her to be destitute, he wasn't going to do her the disservice of handing her a fortune. That was hard for her to understand when she was a teenager, but later, when she had assumed her role in the foundation and begun to make her own way, Barbara not only understood, she was grateful. In the society she traveled in, she came to know many second- and third-generation heirs and she pitied them. She saw them as dilettantes. Their lives were formless, dedicated only to finding ways to spend their money. Oh, there were exceptions, but Barbara was still glad that she worked for a living.

When she had first taken her place on the board of

directors, the others considered her an honorary member, but Barbara had worked hard to dispel that idea. In her heart, she knew that the position wasn't just a meal ticket. Horace was a cunning administrator who had named a group of bankers, stockbrokers, and lawyers to the board to insure the financial stability of the foundation. Then he had named Barbara to insure his own continued influence after his death. Barbara took her position seriously, knowing that Horace wanted the foundation to help people, not institutions. Sometimes she had to fight the rest of the board to get her way, but she rarely backed off and gradually she won the respect of her colleagues.

Walking along, absorbed in her thoughts about the Center, Barbara failed to notice the rapid footfalls approaching from behind her. Without warning, she was roughly pushed against a streetlight pole and before she could recover, her purse was yanked off her arm. She let out a startled cry as her temple hit the metal pole, then looked up in time to see a denim jacket disappear around the next corner.

"Hey you! Stop! Come back here!" she shouted. Regaining her balance, she pushed herself away from the pole and ran after the thief. Her head was throbbing from the collision, but she was too startled and angry to stop and wonder if she was seriously injured.

Running in her high-heeled shoes was awkward, but Barbara gave chase anyway, rounding the corner in time to see the denim jacket disappear down an alley. If she had been thinking calmly and rationally, she might have asked herself exactly what she planned to do if she caught up with the thief, but at the moment, the only thought that occurred to her was that she couldn't let him get away.

Running down the street, she nearly collided with a

foot patrolman who was stepping out of the bakery. "He grabbed my purse!" she gasped, hardly breaking her stride. "He went down that alley. Wearing a denim jacket." The policeman broke into a run with the confidence of one accustomed to sudden emergencies. He took off ahead of Barbara and reached the alley before her.

The passageway cut through the center of the block and came out on the other side. Barbara followed the policeman as his lead widened. She was becoming winded and her footing was uncertain in the narrow, trash-littered passages. She caught up with him when he stopped at the end of the alley and looked up and down the street.

"That him?" the officer asked, pointing to a man in a denim jacket near a car at the curb. He was tall and sturdily built, with short, wavy brown hair. Barbara peered at him. He seemed taller than the man who had pushed her, but she couldn't be sure. She had only caught a glimpse of his back. Then she noticed that the man was using a bent coat hanger to break into the car.

"It must be," Barbara puffed.

The policeman approached the would-be car thief. "Do you have any identification?" he asked. The man at the car looked startled then annoyed.

"It's inside the car—along with my keys," he answered curtly. "I'm not stealing this car, if that's what you think." Barbara came up beside the policeman and took a good look at the man.

"Is he the one, ma'am?"

"I can't be sure," Barbara said. "I only caught a glimpse of him.

"Could I have your name and address, sir?" the policeman asked formally.

"Morgan Newman," the man replied irritably.

"Would it be too much to ask what I'm being accused of?" He gave Barbara a look that made her want to hide behind the policeman.

"Officer, maybe this is a mistake," Barbara said. The man's eyes fell on her and she had the sudden feeling that he couldn't possibly be the one. "I don't see my purse anywhere around here."

"He probably threw it away when he saw he was being chased," the policeman said. "We'll search the alley."

"Officer, if you haven't recognized my name, let me warn you that you will be making trouble for yourself if you continue to harass me," Morgan Newman said ominously.

For the first time, the policeman looked unsure of himself. There was an edge of authority in Newman's voice that carried a distinct message that he was not to be toyed with. The policeman removed his walkie-talkie from his belt and radioed headquarters.

"Could I have your social security number, sir?" He repeated the number to the dispatcher, and the three stood eyeing one another suspiciously while he waited for a reply. After a few uncomfortable moments the radio crackled an inconvenient answer.

"I'm sorry, sir. The computer is off line. I can't verify your identity here. I'm going to have to ask you to come down to the station."

"The hell I will!" Newman snapped. "I am not a purse snatcher or a car thief. I'm making a note of your badge number, officer, and you'll be hearing from your superiors about this outrageous behavior!" He turned back to the car door and started fishing furiously with the bent hanger again. The policeman radioed for a squad car.

"I'm sorry, but I'm going to have to take you to the station. Please put your hands on the hood of the car and spread out your feet."

"What? I will not!"

In a single smooth motion that startled Barbara as much as it did Newman, the policeman grabbed Newman's wrists and handcuffed them behind his back before he could react. At first Barbara thought he was going to lash out in anger, but a deadly calm descended over him. His jaws tightened and he stood silently, glaring at her and the policeman.

"You have the right to remain silent . . ." the policeman began.

"I'm going to have plenty to say when I get hold of your superior," Newman said angrily.

"Officer, maybe he isn't the one," Barbara interjected uncomfortably. "He really doesn't seem right."

"We'll take him down to the station and run his fingerprints," the officer replied. "He's got no identification on him and with his breaking into this car, it's just standard procedure."

Barbara rode to the police station in the front seat while Newman remained silent and sullen in the back. Her head was throbbing and her stomach felt a little queasy, but she chalked it up to the bump, the chase, and the excitement of the incident. She glanced back through the wire screen at Newman several times, but his expression was so hostile that she didn't attempt any communication with him.

Her uncomfortable suspicion that the arrest was a mistake was growing. The name, Morgan Newman, rang a vague bell in Barbara's mind, but as a newcomer to Chicago she wasn't quite sure where she'd heard it. Despite his denim jacket and jeans, she could see that he was no mugger. His jacket was impeccably pressed and his jeans were clean and unwrinkled. His haircut was neat and well styled, emphasizing his high fore-head and clean, strong jawline, and she soon noticed that he was wearing a wristwatch that probably cost more than a month's pay for the neighborhood. He carried himself with authority, and even in the humil-iating position of being handcuffed in the back of a police car, he seemed to be in command of the situa-tion.

At the police station, Barbara was directed to a bench and asked to wait for someone to take her statement. Sitting down, she leaned her head back against the cool wall and closed her eyes, but that turned out to be a mis-take. The sensation of queasiness was increasing, and the room seemed to reel. Barbara snapped her head back up to get her bearings. Moving too quickly also seemed to be a mistake.

Morgan Newman was led in, still in handcuffs, and directed to sit next to a desk. As the foot patrolman who had made the arrest sat down at his typewriter and started to fill out his report, Barbara got up and headed toward him. She walked carefully, trying to protect her aching head from the shock of her feet hitting the floor.

"Excuse me, officer, but do I have to stay here much longer? I really need to get home," she said politely.

"It will be just a few minutes until I can get your state-ment, ma'am."

Barbara had turned to go back to her bench when the chief of police came into the room. She looked over her shoulder to see Morgan Newman watching her intently. His brow was furrowed and he seemed to be worried about what he saw. Barbara wondered if she was look-ing as bad as his face seemed to indicate.

"Morgan! What on earth are you doing here? In hand-cuffs? What is this, a surprise inspection?"

Morgan's attention snapped away from Barbara and

focused on the police chief. "Nothing of the kind, Bob," Morgan said with a considerable edge of disgust in his voice. "It seems I'm being accused of snatching purses and stealing cars."

The police chief's eyes widened as he looked from Morgan to the policeman who had made the arrest. "Connors, I'd like to speak to you in my office." The two policemen went into the private office at the end of the squad room and closed the door, leaving Morgan still handcuffed. Barbara heard voices being raised, and moments later both the patrolman and his chief returned. The patrolman's face was flushed and he looked distinctly uncomfortable, as he immediately uncuffed the "thief."

"I'm really sorry about this, Morgan," the police chief said. "Connors is new on the beat. He's only been in the city for a few weeks."

"I suppose no harm has been done," he replied gruffly. Barbara got up and came back to the desk.

"I'm sorry if I've caused you trouble," she said, then turned to the policemen. "Can I go now?"

"We'll still want to fill out a report on your stolen purse, ma'am," the patrolman answered.

"I may be able to offer some assistance," Morgan interjected in a softer tone. Now that his identity had been established, he seemed to be getting over his pique at being arrested. "I think I saw a man in a jean jacket come running out of that alley just before you arrested me. I would have mentioned it earlier, but I didn't think of it until after we were in the squad car, and by then I wasn't feeling very helpful." He smiled and got up to offer Barbara his seat next to the booking desk. "You'd better sit down here. I'm afraid I didn't start out in the best of moods tonight. I locked my keys in my car and I was engrossed in trying to get the car open when the purse snatcher came by."

"I can't say how sorry we are that we inconvenienced you, Morgan," the police chief said, obviously more concerned about Morgan's temper than Barbara's purse. "It's not every day that we arrest the chairman of the Police Appropriations Committee for purse snatching. I'll have a squad car take you back to your car and help you get into it."

"Well, don't be in such a rush, Bob," Morgan said. "Maybe I can help give a description of the real crook." The hostility in Morgan's demeanor had gradually faded away. He was in complete control now, and Barbara thought that she might even have found him charming if her head hadn't hurt so much. She blinked several times, trying to get the room to settle down around her, and held on to the edge of the desk for support so hard that her knuckles were turning white.

"Are you all right?" The voice seemed to be coming from a long way off and she wasn't sure who was speaking. She tried to nod her head, but she seemed to have lost control of her neck muscles. For a long moment she lost contact with the room around her, then awoke to find herself lying on the floor with several concerned faces bent over her.

"What's your name? Are you allergic to any medication? What is your address? Is there anybody we should contact?" She had to strain to sort out the questions and make sense of them.

"Barbara Danbury," she said with difficulty. Her mouth was dry and her tongue didn't want to form the words. "I live at Twenty-one-twenty-one Forty-first Street, apartment five-A." She tried to sit up, but gentle hands forced her back down. "I'm okay. I just want to go home," she said weakly.

"You just stay put," a kind voice replied. "We've called an ambulance to take you to the emergency room. That's a nasty bump you've got on your head."

"But I've got to go home. Bogey's been inside all day. He hasn't been fed. I've got to go home and take care of him." Barbara tried to get up again, but failed.

"Who's Bogey?"

"My dog. Please, would someone call my landlord and ask him to take care of Bogey?"

"We'll take care of it, don't worry." Barbara managed to focus her eyes well enough to see that it was Morgan Newman speaking to her.

Barbara relaxed then, resigning herself to her helpless position. Everything seemed confused. She felt like she ought to be doing something, but she couldn't remember what. "I should have listened to Ossie," she mumbled before she let go of consciousness once again.

# Chapter Two

❦

Barbara awoke in a strange bed with sheets that felt stiff and coarse. She opened her eyes, and slowly sat up to take in her surroundings. The room was sparely furnished, and a slight odor of disinfectant hung in the air. Putting her hand up to her face, Barbara found a square gauze bandage on her temple.

"You're awake?"

Barbara was suddenly aware of her roommate, a middle-aged woman with frowzy brown-and-gray hair, sagging jowls, and a double chin. The woman was propped up in bed on several pillows, observing Barbara with a look of almost morbid curiosity.

"I think so," Barbara answered uncertainly. "Where am I?"

"City General," her roommate answered. "They brought you in here last night—out colder than a mackerel. I'm glad you're awake, I want to watch TV." She picked up the remote control for the television set and started going from channel to channel.

Barbara felt a slightly cold draft on her back where

the hospital gown gaped open. She noticed the hospital identification bracelet on her wrist and read it out loud. "Barbara Danbury, E.R. admission, concussion."

"You having trouble remembering who you are?"

"No, I know who I am, but how I got here is a little fuzzy," Barbara replied. "I was at the police station and I remember somebody saying something about calling an ambulance."

"I'm Maudine Fortney. I'm here for a gall bladder. Got stones the size of golf balls," the other woman said with pride.

Barbara sincerely hoped that Maudine would get interested in a television program and spare her the details of the operation. Her head was aching slightly and she didn't feel like comparing medical histories. She reached up and touched her bandage again.

"Your old man knock you around?" Maudine asked in a tone that held more curiosity than concern.

"I was mugged."

Maudine turned back to the television with a bored, "Oh," as if a mugging were too commonplace to warrant her attention. She started changing channels again, settling for a moment or two of this quiz show or talk show—always ending up dissatisfied and turning to something else. After tiring of an "I Love Lucy" rerun, she turned to "Good Morning Windy City," a talk and news program.

"And now to city hall for a live report from Celia Caron on the latest furor over Councilman Morgan Newman," the host said. The name caught Barbara's attention.

The scene shifted to a crowded corridor in city hall. "Thank you, Jack," Celia Caron said. "We're waiting here to speak with Councilman Newman in person . . ."

Maudine picked up the remote control and started to change the channel.

"No, please, leave it on. I'd like to see this," Barbara said. Maudine shrugged and set the control back down.

Morgan stepped out of a door and faced the crowd of reporters in the hall. He was dressed in a dark brown suit and subtly-striped tie now, but Barbara couldn't mistake his handsome face—the same face that had bent over her with such concern last night when she had passed out at the police station. He was relaxed and completely at ease in front of the cameras, and there was something in his casual manner that inspired trust.

"Mr. Newman," a reporter called out, sticking a microphone under his nose. "Is it true that you were arrested last night?"

Morgan made a face as if he hadn't wanted to answer that question, but he followed the grimace with an open smile. "Yes, it's absolutely true—unfortunately."

"What were the charges?" another reporter called out.

"Purse snatching," Morgan said with a broad smile. The reporters broke out into pandemonium, all trying to get their own questions through. Morgan held up his hands for silence.

"If you'll all be patient, I'd like to make a brief statement. Then I'll answer all the questions we have time for." The reporters settled down to listen.

"First, I'd like to say that while we of the city council have often been accused of picking the taxpayers' pockets, we haven't resorted to snatching purses on the street—yet. I don't think you'll have to worry about that unless Councilman Baker's tax limitation plan goes through." Morgan paused while the reporters laughed at his joke.

"The arrest was a simple mistake," he continued. "It

was something that could have happened to anybody. I have no intention of filing false arrest charges against the officer involved or anyone else. Now, if any of you have questions . . ."

"Mr. Newman, how is it that a well-known councilman can be arrested by 'mistake'?" a serious young man with a spiral notebook rather than a microphone asked suspiciously.

"A purse was snatched just a few blocks from where I was. Apparently the thief was wearing a jacket much like my own. You might say I was handy and fit the description."

"But surely, Mr. Newman, when you showed your identification . . ." the reporter pressed.

"First, let me say that no one should be exempt from a criminal investigation just because he can show identification proving that he's an important person. I'm embarrassed to say, however, that I didn't have any identification on me. I had put my wallet in my glove compartment, and then, absent-mindedly, I locked my keys in my car. When the officer came along I was using a coat hanger to break into my own car. I'm afraid it looked very suspicious."

"But Mr. Newman, with that expensive new computer system the police have, shouldn't they have been able to confirm your identity and ownership of the car with just your social security and license plate numbers?" the reporter continued doggedly.

Morgan chuckled. "Yes, that's the way it's supposed to work, but Murphy's Law was operating—you know, anything that can go wrong, will go wrong. The computer was off-line. The officer had no choice but to take me in."

"Yet, you have no criticisms of the police?"

"I think I'll leave that to your Mr. Feeny at the *Tele-*

graph," Morgan said humorously. "Now why don't we let someone else get in a question?"

A woman from one of the television stations was ready. "Mr. Newman, since you're the chairman of the Police Appropriations Committee, could this incident have some ramifications on this year's budget?"

Morgan smiled. It was clear that he had been waiting for this question. "As a matter of fact, yes. Actually, I think it would be a great idea if we could arrange to have the whole city council arrested periodically. I learned things about the operation of the Chicago Police Department that I never could have learned working through the department hierarchy. The computer was off-line because the operator had taken a break. Since we can't expect the city computer operators to give up coffee breaks, it follows that the computer is understaffed. I'm going to recommend an increase in the personnel budget for that department."

"What about the real purse snatcher?" someone else asked.

"Well, the most positive thing I can say about him is that he has excellent taste in clothing," Morgan quipped.

The reporters laughed appreciatively again. "But was he apprehended?"

"Not to my knowledge, but you'll have to talk to the police about that. Now, ladies and gentlemen, if you'll excuse me, I have a committee meeting to attend." Morgan smiled charmingly, disappeared through a door, and the scene shifted back to the television studio.

Barbara lay back down in the bed, fascinated by what she had just seen. She tried to reconcile the smooth, poised person on television with the man she had been with last night. The evening's events were jumbled in her mind, but even so, it was hard to believe that this was the same person. Barbara was curious about this man. Judging by the media coverage, he was more important than the average councilman, and she wanted to know more about him.

"Have you lived in Chicago long?" she asked Maudine.

"All my life and then some," the woman answered.

"Do you know anything about Morgan Newman?"

Maudine laughed out loud. "Just what I see on the tube and read in the papers. You new around here?"

"Yes, I've only been in town a few weeks. I was curious about him. The press seems to be making an awfully big deal about a silly little arrest."

"When Morgan Newman blows his nose, three reporters fight over the tissue before it hits the waste-basket," Maudine commented with a laugh.

"Why do they make such a big fuss over him?" Barbara asked.

"Because he's so active, I guess, not to mention handsome. You can't pick up a newspaper in this town without reading about his latest project, of the new ordinance he pushed through the city council, or who he took to a benefit dance. He's done a lot of good for the city. I'd vote for him—if I lived in his ward."

"Doesn't he take his wife to benefit dances?" Barbara asked obliquely.

"He's not married—you really *are* new in town. Half the gossip columnists can't write about anything except who Morgan Newman goes out with. He's probably the most eligible bachelor in the city."

Barbara laughed. "Well, don't keep me in suspense. Whom does he date?"

"Everybody," Maudine replied. "Everybody who's

beautiful and glamorous, that is. I'm afraid I'm not in his little black book."

"Don't feel bad, neither am I."

"You look a lot closer to his type than me."

"Not anymore. I was the one who had him arrested last night."

Maudine sat up and took a closer look at Barbara. "No kidding? You actually met him?"

"Sort of, but it wasn't very sociable."

"Wait till the bridge club hears about this," Maudine said.

Just then a young doctor came into the room. He approached Barbara with a serious expression that seemed to compensate for his youthful looks. "Ms. Danbury, how are you feeling this morning?" He pulled the curtain to isolate Barbara's bed from Maudine's.

"My head still hurts, but other than that I seem to be all right," Barbara answered.

"I'm Doctor Carter. May I call you Barbara?" When she nodded, he continued. "Good, Barbara, now I want you to look at this light." He took a penlight out of his pocket and examined her pupils. "How many fingers do you see?" he asked, holding up his index finger.

"One," she answered.

After a thorough examination, Doctor Carter said, "Everything seems to be in order, though you may have a headache for several days. You don't seem to have suffered anything worse than a mild concussion, so I'll sign the release forms and you can check out today. We just wanted to keep you over night for observation."

"Thank you, Doctor Carter. Is there a phone around here where I can call someone to come get me? My purse was stolen last night and I'm afraid I don't have money for a cab."

"Just go down to the nurses' station, they'll help you out."

"And where are my clothes?"

Dr. Carter smiled. "In the closet. Now, I'll give you a prescription for the headache, but you shouldn't drive a car while you're taking this." He wrote it out and handed the slip of paper to Barbara. "If you have any problems, like dizziness or fainting, or if your headache doesn't go away in a few days, call me and we'll bring you back for some more X rays. Now it's your turn, Maudine," he said as he got up and went around to the other side of the curtain.

"I'm starving to death, Doctor," Maudine complained. "Can't a body get anything to eat in this hospital?"

"You know the rules, Maudine—nothing to eat for eight hours before surgery."

After Barbara had dressed and said good-bye to Maudine, she went down to the nurses' station, where she was able to use the phone to call Brad Allen—the one person in Chicago she knew well enough to depend on in a situation like this. As she took the elevator down to the lobby to wait for him, she knew she was due for a lecture on walking the streets alone. Brad had been offering her rides ever since they'd started working together, but Barbara had always refused, partly to prove to Brad that she wasn't afraid of the neighborhood and partly because she enjoyed the walk.

When she'd started working with Brad, proving that she wasn't too delicate for the neighborhood had been very important to Barbara. He'd made no secret of the fact that he didn't want her involved in the Center; it had been his idea and he wanted to run it himself.

He had first walked into her office at the Calvin Foundation wearing cut-off jeans and a ragged T-shirt, and

Barbara's initial impression of Brad Allen had been determined by his aggressive personality rather than his tremendous talent. When he'd slammed the dog-eared folder containing his proposal for the Thirty-seventh Street Center down on her desk, Barbara had been tempted to use her intercom and call for help. The brooding expression on his dark face had increased the apprehension Barbara felt as she looked at him. He was short, but powerfully built, and from his looks he might have been a weight lifter or a boxer. Barbara soon learned that his physique was a result of his single passion in life—dancing.

"What's this?" Barbara had asked, returning his stare in spite of her qualms.

"It's a proposal that you are probably going to throw in the trash as soon as I walk out of here," he'd said belligerently.

"No, I'll look it over and give you a call in a few days," Barbara had replied evenly. "If you could leave your name and number with my secretary . . ."

"Since you'll probably throw that proposal—which I've worked very hard on—away as soon as I walk out of here, I have no intention of leaving. You can read it right now."

"I'm sorry, but I'm very busy. I assure you that I'll give your proposal equal consideration with every other one I have. Just leave your number with my secretary."

Brad had scowled and sat down in the chair opposite Barbara's desk, crossing his legs and folding his arms over his chest.

"Excuse me . . . Mr. Allen," Barbara had said, reading his name from the top of the proposal. "But camping in my office is not going to do your proposal any good."

"I've been thrown out of the offices of nearly every

charitable foundation east of the Mississippi," he'd said slowly. "If you'd like to try it, I'll add you to the list. Unless you intend to remove me physically, you might as well read the proposal."

Picking up the papers angrily, she'd started to read and before she finished Barbara knew she had a good idea in her hands. But it wasn't the type of proposal that the board of directors was going to be convinced to support easily.

"Mr. Allen," she'd begun. "I can see that this idea has merit, but—"

"Spare me. I already know all the 'buts'—but this isn't our kind of project, but we've never done anything like this before, but money is tight. Why don't you come out and say what you mean—but this project would be spending money on people who need it instead of rich kids who want to go to an Ivy League college or high-society types who want a symphony hall in their community. This project would be doing more for the arts than six pre-med scholarships or ten symphony halls."

Barbara had stood and leaned over the desk, looking straight into Brad's eyes. "I wasn't going to say anything of the kind," she said steadily, ignoring his bitterness. "But I need details. For example, who would do the teaching?"

He'd held Barbara's stare for several moments without flinching before he spoke. "I would. I'd also hire other instructors for the drama and vocal classes."

Barbara had taken Brad's proposal to the board and pushed it through, using every bit of leverage she had. The weak link she saw in the plan, however, was Brad's personality. He was an artist. He'd danced lead parts with half a dozen professional ballet companies but he was totally lacking in diplomacy. His idea of cooperation was for everyone to do exactly what he wanted.

Barbara simply couldn't see him in charge of a project that would require the cooperation of a diverse group of people.

So Barbara had dealt herself into the project. The Center would have Calvin Foundation funds on the condition that Barbara would have administrative control during its establishing period. Brad had been openly hostile at first; he didn't want Barbara meddling with his plans. But after a week, his hostility turned to grudging tolerance, and as Brad learned to respect Barbara's administrative talents, she was discovering that all Brad's talents didn't lie in performance. He was a marvel at working with the children. His gruffness didn't fool them for a moment; he was like a pied piper, drawing them into the Center. In addition, he was handy and willing to do almost anything that needed to be done, including most of the remodeling work on the old storefront space that they had turned into the Center.

As the Center took shape Barbara realized that Brad *was* capable of running the project without her intervention. But when she'd talked of handing it over to him and returning to New York, he had asked her to stay for a while longer. Her help in taking care of the administrative duties while he was setting up programs was proving invaluable.

Barbara looked up to see Brad standing in front of her in a pair of sweatpants and a T-shirt bearing the legend "Dancers Do It Gracefully." His face was a dark cloud.

"How many times have I offered you a ride home?" he said irritably. "But no, you've got to walk. You are the stubbornest woman I've ever known. I hope you're satisfied!"

"Thank you, Brad," Barbara said quietly.

"Thanks for nothing. From now on when I offer a ride, you're going to take it," he said angrily.

"Thanks for caring," Barbara replied evenly.

Brad only harrumphed. "Let's get going. I have a class at eleven."

"This is nothing to get excited about," Barbara said defensively as they walked out to the car. "It was my own fault. I was walking along, daydreaming, and my purse was slung over my arm like a fruit ready to pick. I'll just have to be more careful from now on."

"You're lucky all he wanted was your purse," Brad said as he opened the car door for Barbara.

"Brad, don't go making a mountain out of a mole-hill."

"Bunch of kids showed up this morning asking for you," Brad said, changing the subject abruptly.

"Oh, good. Was one of them a Munchkin con man named Ossie?"

"I think so. I'm putting the bunch of them in the Junior Creative Movement section. Most of them have the coordination of a bunch of hound-dog puppies, but there was one girl in the group who may show some promise."

Brad guided the car through traffic back to the neighborhood and they discussed their work at the Center until he stopped in front of Barbara's building.

"Thanks for coming to get me," Barbara said as she stepped out onto the sidewalk. "I'm just going to take a shower and change my clothes, then I'll come down to the Center."

"Why don't you take the day off? You could use the rest."

"Phooey, I got plenty of rest last night. I'll just walk over when I get ready."

Brad looked frustrated as Barbara shut the car door and went inside to get the passkey from her landlord.

"Mr. Fordson?" she called out. "Mr. Fordson, are you home?" A bit of yelling was usually necessary because of the man's hearing problem.

The door opened a crack as old Mr. Fordson peeked out with the chain still fastened. His rheumy eyes lit up as he spied his favorite tenant. "Oh, Barbara," he said as he removed the chain and opened the door. "What can I do for you?"

"I need the passkey to get into my apartment, since mine was stolen. Oh, and how is Bogey?"

Mr. Fordson turned to shuffle back to his kitchen, where he kept the keys, without answering her question. That was normal, as it was generally necessary to ask a question two or three times before getting an answer from the old man. Barbara stepped inside the door and pulled it shut. "Bogey," she called out quietly. "You here, boy?" There was no answer.

Mr. Fordson returned with the key. "You lock your keys inside?" he inquired as he handed it to her.

"No, my purse was snatched. Is Bogey still upstairs?"

"If that's where you left him." Mr. Fordson looked puzzled.

"Didn't someone call you last night and ask you to take him out and feed him for me? I had to spend the night at the hospital."

"If anybody called me, I didn't hear it," Mr. Fordson replied. "I went out to the Senior's Dance down at the Y last night. I ought to do that more often." He chuckled with pleasure at the memory of the night before.

"I'd better run upstairs then," Barbara said nervously. "Poor Bogey's been alone since yesterday morning. I'll be lucky if he hasn't shredded my sofa."

She hurried up the stairs and opened her door.

"Bogey, Bogey," she called out. "Come on, baby. I'm sorry I left you all alone." She made a quick circuit of the apartment without finding her dog. After checking under the furniture she was distressed that she still hadn't found him.

"Where are you, boy?" she said quietly. Not only was her dog not in evidence, she couldn't find any signs that he had relieved himself anywhere on the floor, which would have been expected after his twenty-four hour seclusion. After several minutes of worried searching, Barbara found the window overlooking the fire escape open just wide enough for a Yorkshire terrier to squeeze through—if he could jump up on the sill. It seemed an unlikely feat, but Bogey was nowhere to be found.

A sick feeling washed over her. She didn't remember leaving the window open, but the fact was that Bogey was gone. He had always been an apartment dog; Barbara could only imagine him frightened and hungry, huddled in an alley, or worst of all, run over by a car.

She was about to go searching outside when the telephone rang.

"Ms. Danbury?" a feminine voice asked. "Hold for Mr. Newman, please."

There was an interval of annoying recorded music on the phone, then Morgan clicked in.

"Ms. Danbury?" he asked.

"Yes?"

"Could you do me a favor and come to my office to claim this ferocious little wolf of yours?"

"You have Bogey?" she asked with relief.

"Yes, or maybe it would be more apt to say he has us."

"But how did you end up with him?"

"I couldn't reach your landlord last night. You seemed so worried about him that I called one of my aides and had him pick Bogey up. I'd really appreciate it if you could come get him as soon as possible."

"Has he been any trouble?"

Morgan gave out an odd laugh. "It depends on how you define trouble. I suppose the cleaning lady will be able to take care of the spot on the carpet in my office, but it will probably take a week or two for the teeth marks in Ron's ankle to heal."

"Bogey bit someone? But he never bites!"

"Never until last night," Morgan corrected her. "But I suppose we can forgive a small dog for biting a stranger in his home when his owner isn't there. Considering Bogey's size in relation to Ron, I guess you might even call it courageous. However, Ron informs me that he isn't coming into my office until I get rid of the 'vicious' animal."

"I'll be there as soon as I can," Barbara said with a laugh.

"I'll be waiting," Morgan replied.

# Chapter Three

Showering quickly, Barbara changed into a beige linen suit and blue silk blouse. The bandage at her temple was far from attractive, but she took care with her makeup, applying an earthy brown eye shadow to bring out the warm tones of her eyes and a deep red lipstick to add a bright focus to her otherwise subdued color scheme. Then she brushed her springy red curls forward to partially obscure the bandage, and made a quick check in the full-length mirror on the back of her bedroom door.

The suit was dressier than the clothes she had become accustomed to wearing lately, but her errand to city hall seemed to call for a more stylish outfit. Her spirits were high, now that she knew that Bogey was safe, and a chance for a second meeting with the fascinating man she had seen on television that morning was a prospect that for some reason pleased her beyond the relief she felt for her pet's safety.

After putting a comb and a few basic makeup items in

a bone-colored leather clutch bag, she set out for city hall with a stop at her bank to replace the money she had lost in her purse.

The bank took longer than she had expected, since she was required to fill out several forms to report her missing checkbook and identification, but by noontime she was standing before Morgan's secretary in the outer office of his suite.

"Ms. Danbury?" the secretary asked with a smile. "I'm Sylvia Chaney. Mr. Newman will be with you shortly."

"I'm very sorry Bogey has been making a nuisance of himself," Barbara apologized. "He's not used to being with strangers."

"Mr. Newman is with someone at the moment," the secretary said with a polite smile. "You can go in and get your dog as soon as he's through. Would you like a cup of coffee?"

"Yes, thank you," she replied before taking a seat near a large potted Schefflera plant. Barbara took a long look at Sylvia as she went over to the coffee pot. The secretary was just the type of girl Barbara would have expected to be working for a man like Morgan Newman. She was somewhere in her mid-twenties with shoulder-length blonde hair that practically sparkled in the bright office light, and the short, pleated skirt of her mauve suit showed off her shapely legs. A gold charm bracelet jingled at her wrist, and as she handed Barbara the coffee, Barbara noticed her perfect manicure.

Barbara was amused at herself for taking such an interest in the young woman. She thought that she had grown out of the habit of casing the competition long ago, and told herself that she had no reason to believe Morgan's secretary was anything but an employee. And even if this sparkling post-teenager were something more, it was none of her concern.

"He's really very cute," Sylvia said, startling Barbara out of her private thoughts.

"What?"

"Bogey. He's really cute. I wish I could have a dog like that, but my husband is allergic to animal hair."

Barbara laughed out loud with a relief that surprised and embarrassed her. "I've always said that Bogey is better than having a husband," she joked, trying to cover her reaction. "I have to feed him and pick up after him, but he doesn't have any laundry and he never gives me any back talk."

Sylvia laughed with Barbara. "Next time Steve gives me a hard time I'm going to threaten to get rid of him and get a Yorkie," she said. "That should whip him into line."

One of several office doors opened and a young man in a three-piece suit stepped out. "I need ten copies of this by three, Sylvia," he said peremptorily as he placed a sheaf of papers on the corner of her desk. Barbara thought she saw a wave of resentment pass across the secretary's face. She couldn't put her finger on it, but there was something unpleasant about the young man. As Barbara watched him talking to Sylvia, she decided that it was because of his eyes, they were hard and cold. Even if he smiled, Barbara felt that his eyes wouldn't follow suit.

"Councilman Newman may be tied up for a while," he said as he noticed Barbara waiting. "Perhaps I could help you. I'm Ron Caldwell, Mr. Newman's aide." He extended his hand to Barbara and as he smiled, she saw that she had been right. Only the corners of his mouth turned up; his eyes retained their humorless glint.

She accepted his handshake, repelled to find his palm cold and clammy.

"Mr. Caldwell . . . you must be the one my dog bit. I'm really very sorry. He's never done that before. I'll be glad to cover any medical care you may need."

Caldwell looked even more uncomfortable and Barbara secretly decided that Bogey had shown excellent judgment when he had bitten the man. "Oh, it was nothing serious," he said flatly. "Just a few little scratches. He's had his shots, hasn't he?"

"Of course," Barbara replied, thinking that she ought to ask if Caldwell had had *his* shots. The idea that this man had entered her apartment—even if it had been to rescue Bogey—was making her uncomfortable. "I suppose you got into my apartment through the window."

"Oh, uh, sure." He answered evasively.

"I'm not usually so careless as to leave a window unlocked," she said.

"Uh, I guess it was a good thing," Caldwell replied, glancing around as if to see who was listening. Suddenly he seemed eager to get away from Barbara. "I'm going to be busy for a while, Sylvia. "Hold my calls," he said as he disappeared.

Sylvia leafed through the papers he had deposited on her desk. "And he expects me to correct his grammar and spelling while I'm at it," she grumbled.

Another office door opened and a portly, bald man in a pin-striped suit stepped out. He turned back to the open door for a final comment. "Thank you, Mr. Newman. I can't tell you what your concern for our problems means to us."

Morgan stepped through the door and put a friendly hand on the man's shoulder. "I think I should be thanking you," he said. "The council can only help if citizens' groups like yours keep us informed of what needs to be done. I'll be bringing up your problem at the next council meeting."

Morgan stood in his office door as the man made his way out. When his eyes fell on Barbara, they brightened and his smile grew wider, making her pulse quicken unaccountably as she returned his smile. "Ms. Danbury, you're looking much better than the last time I saw you. I hope you're feeling better?"

"I'm fine—just a little bit of a headache. It really wasn't very serious," she replied, nervously touching the bandage at her temple.

"Come on in. I think I can arrange a reunion for you." Before Barbara got to the door, Morgan turned to Sylvia with some instructions, and his manner revealed a great deal more tact than Ron Caldwell had shown. The difference wasn't so much in his choice of words, but in the way his authority lacked the arrogance his aide had.

When Barbara entered the room, she could see that Morgan's office reflected the power of the man who occupied it. The glass wall behind his desk looked out over the city and the sheer curtains were drawn, making the view of the Chicago skyline hazy and indistinct like a fairy tale landscape of towers and turrets. The deep-pile beige carpet was springy underfoot and soft music played from a hidden speaker. One wall was occupied by built-in bookcases filled with official-looking volumes. His huge, polished mahogany desk dominated the center of the room, its surface clear except for the stacked "IN" and "OUT" baskets and the small Yorkshire terrier sitting in the middle of the blotter. Bogy jumped up and danced from foot to foot, whimpering with joy, as soon as he spied Barbara.

"Bogey!" she exclaimed as she scooped him up and hugged him. "I'll bet you thought I was never coming back." She laughed as he squirmed and licked her face.

"I'm sorry about your carpet, Mr. Newman," Barbara said. "I'll be glad to pay to have it cleaned."

"I'll forget about the carpet if you'll call me Morgan and have lunch with me today," he said, smiling with a warmth that made Barbara feel as if she were with an old friend. "I don't think we can blame this little fellow. I think he was just nervous about being in a strange place when I brought him in this morning. After he got used to the surroundings, he was a perfect gentleman." Morgan reached out and rubbed Bogey's head.

"Except for biting Mr. Caldwell," Barbara said.

"Sometimes I want to do that, too," Morgan chuckled. "But Ron has his talents, so I keep him around."

"I suppose I could manage lunch, if I can take Bogey home and feed him first. He must be starved."

"I don't think he's all that hungry. I took him home with me last night and he dined on leftover boeuf bourguignon."

"Oh dear, I hope he'll still settle for kibble," Barbara said with mock alarm.

"My car is downstairs in the parking garage," Morgan said. "We can drop Bogey off at your place on our way." He pulled his car keys out of his pocket and held them up. "I've discovered a wonderful way of getting into a locked car—use the key."

They had the elevator to themselves on the way down to the garage. Barbara carried Bogey tucked under her arm. "I'm really sorry about last night," Barbara said as the doors closed.

"What do you have to be sorry about?"

"I caused you a lot of trouble—first pointing you out as the thief, then with Bogey and all."

"I wouldn't worry about it very much," Morgan replied. "To tell the truth, I'm kind of ashamed of myself. If I hadn't been so surly, I might have worked something out with the policeman before we got to the point of an arrest. And I'm really ashamed of myself for not noticing that you were hurt until we got to the station."

"I didn't notice until then, either," Barbara replied. "And I can understand why you were upset. Locking keys in your car and then getting arrested isn't exactly a four-star evening."

"Well, I should have kept calm. In my line of work you can't afford to lose your temper in public." The elevator doors slid open on the garage level, and Morgan put an arm around Barbara to guide her to the car. She was pleasantly aware of his height, an easy three or four inches more than her own, even with the heels she was wearing. As he opened the car door for her, he flourished the keys to show his skill at the common method of opening a locked car. With a laugh, she slid into the passenger seat and settled Bogey on her lap.

"So," Morgan asked as he drove the car into traffic, "why does a beautiful and obviously cultured woman like yourself live in a neighborhood like Thirty-seventh Street? And don't tell me you can't afford anything better."

"My, my," Barbara chuckled. "Do you always ask such personal questions? I don't know if I should answer that."

"You don't have to, but I'm dying of curiosity and if I drop dead in the Chicago noon traffic, we're both in trouble."

"I took an apartment near my job," Barbara answered.

"And what job is that?" Morgan asked, giving her a sidelong glance.

"Well, I'm only here temporarily. I'm representing the Calvin Foundation's interests in the Thirty-seventh

Street Center for the Performing Arts. I really live in New York."

"The Thirty-seventh Street Center—that's the youth center being set up by that ballet dancer, what's his name?"

"Brad Allen," Barbara supplied. "I'm happy to know you've heard of us."

"I haven't heard much, actually. We didn't have too much to do with it in the council because it's all privately funded. I just remember something about a zoning variance to put a school in that area."

Barbara sighed. "That's our trouble—getting the word out. If we were doing this in a smaller city, the media would be crawling all over us. But in Chicago, you've got to be a natural disaster or a councilman to get any attention."

Morgan pulled up at the curb outside Barbara's apartment and came around to open her car door. When Bogey was settled on his favorite cushion near the refrigerator, she returned to the street where Morgan waited in the car.

"By the way, I saw you on television this morning," Barbara said as she got back in the car.

Morgan gave her an almost sheepish smile. "I suppose that convinced you that I'm a complete hypocrite—after seeing what actually happened last night."

"No," Barbara protested. "I was really impressed with the way you handled it."

"Where would you like to go for lunch?" Morgan asked, changing the subject.

"It doesn't really matter. I'm sure you know where to go around here much better than I do."

"In that case, let's go to The Newsroom. They have the best sandwich board I know."

"The Newsroom? It doesn't sound like a place to eat."

"It's on the street floor of the WRRG-TV building. That's how it got its name. It's a favorite with a lot of media types, but since they all got their shot at me this morning, I think we can go there without too much danger of interruption."

The Newsroom was crowded with people sharing loud conversations along with their sandwiches and coffee. The hostess led them to a booth near the back of the restaurant ahead of other couples who had been waiting, and a pretty waitress in a snap-brim hat with fake press passes tucked in the band arrived to take their order almost instantaneously. She paid solicitous attention to Morgan, flashing a coy smile at appropriate intervals and leaning over him precariously to fill his water glass and arrange his place setting.

"I see why you like to come here," Barbara said dryly.

"Well, the food is good, too," he replied with a sly smile.

While they were waiting for their sandwiches, several people stopped by the table just to greet Morgan. If Barbara had had anything particularly involved or important to say, she would have had difficulty getting to say it. However, as things were, she didn't mind the interruptions; they gave her a chance to watch Morgan closely without being under observation herself, and she liked what she saw.

There was something very special in Morgan's manner. He had an unusual ability, considering the number of people he spoke with, to make each one feel as if he or she were terribly important to him. If transcribed, the words he said would have sounded bland and impersonal, but when he said them, they were full of warmth and sincerity. He asked some minor personal question about each person who came up to speak to him, and

Barbara marveled that he could remember so many details about so many people.

"I'm afraid you're getting the short shrift here," Morgan said with an apologetic smile as yet another person left them. Reaching across the table, he took her hand, and Barbara realized with embarrassment that she had been absent-mindedly drumming her fingers. "They'll stop dropping by as soon as our lunch arrives."

"That's all right. I suppose I should be cultivating these people myself—to get more publicity for the center."

Morgan's face lit up, and he turned to wave and get the attention of a stocky man with a handlebar moustache. The man came over and shook Morgan's hand.

"George, I'd like you to meet my friend, Barbara Danbury," he said. "Barbara, this is George Leland. He produces "Good Morning Windy City." Barbara is working on the Thirty-seventh Street Center."

George Leland raised an eyebrow. "And what, pray tell, is the Thirty-seventh Street Center? As if you weren't about to tell me."

"You haven't heard about the Thirty-seventh Street Center?" Morgan asked with eyes open in surprise. "A top ballet star like Brad Allen gives up the stage to teach his art to Chicago kids in a storefront on Thirty-seventh Street and "Good Morning Windy City" doesn't know about it?"

If it were possible, George Leland's eyebrow seemed to go even higher. "Ms. Danbury, would you be amenable to having us come out to do a segment for the show? It sounds as if the story has a lot of appeal."

"Why certainly, Mr. Leland," Barbara answered smoothly. "Let me give you the Center's telephone number and you can call to set up an appointment.

We'll make sure that our clumsier students are somewhere else."

"Oh no, that would be cheating," the producer
replied with a chuckle. The waitress arrived with their
sandwiches, and Mr. Leland excused himself after
thanking Morgan for the news tip.

Barbara started to laugh as soon as they were alone.
"Do you always deliver such immediate results?" she
asked.

"I aim to please," Morgan replied with a wink. "But
to tell the truth, I'm glad we have our peace at last so I
can ask you something really important."

"What's that?" Barbara asked between bites of her
sandwich.

"Are you busy Thursday night?"

"It depends on what you have in mind," Barbara
replied playfully. "I've been hearing rumors about your
reputation with women. I don't know if I'm quite in
your league."

"I suppose you've heard all those rumors like, my little black book is February's Book-of-the-Month-Club
selection—in three hardbound volumes," Morgan said
with a mischievous twinkle in his hazel eyes.

"Something like that," she smiled.

"Well, don't believe everything you hear," he said in
a more serious tone. "I can't win no matter what I do. If I
just date one woman, the gossip columnists all say that
I'm 'getting serious' and 'about to pop the question.' If I
date a lot of different women, I'm a playboy. The truth
is, the politicians' social circuit just isn't set up for
single people. I'm expected to bring a date to all those
banquets and benefits, and to be completely honest,
that's what I had in mind for Thursday night. The Clean
Up Our Parks Committee is holding a benefit dinner. It
won't be the intimate evening that I'd prefer to spend

with you, but it could be an opportunity to get better acquainted."

"I know exactly what you mean about being single," Barbara replied. "As a charity administrator, I have to go to a lot of the same kind of functions. Only it's harder for a single woman to scare up a date."

"I shouldn't think you'd have too much trouble," Morgan said with a charming smile.

Barbara laughed. "You don't know who your true friends are until you try to find a date for the Save the Snail Darter wine and cheese party."

"You haven't answered my question."

"Yes," Barbara said positively. "I'd be delighted to go to the Clean Up Our Parks dinner."

"In that case, madame, I am at your disposal should the question of saving the snail darter ever arise," Morgan with mock pomposity.

Barbara smiled back at him. "I believe the snail darter is relatively safe these days," she replied. "But be aware that, sooner or later, I may end up calling in your I.O.U."

"Are you warning me that a date with you may mean entanglements I'm not planning on?" Morgan asked with a gleam in his eyes that said more than his words.

"I suppose I'm taking the same risk," Barbara replied with a similiar expression.

"Life is full of risks—nothing ventured, nothing gained."

"Then here's to peril," Barbara said, raising her coffee cup in a toast.

Morgan chuckled. "Why does it seem like we've made a pact to mount a commando raid and blow up a bridge in enemy territory? I thought I was asking you for a date."

"I don't know. Maybe it just seems a little bit perilous

to agree to go out with a man whose little black book rivals the Manhattan phone directory," Barbara laughed.

"Thousands of women can't all be wrong," Morgan said with a mock sigh. "I must be charming company."

"Maybe you just can't get one woman to go out with you twice," Barbara teased.

"Ah, shot down in the prime of my life," Morgan laughed.

They lingered over a second cup of coffee while the lunch crowd thinned out and faded away. A waitress was conspicuously cleaning off tables all around them when Morgan glanced at his watch.

"I've got a budget committee meeting at two-forty-five," he said apologetically, "so I'm afraid we've got to go. Can I drop you off at home?"

"I'd appreciate it if you'd drop me at the Center. It's just a few blocks from my place. I really should make some kind of appearance at work today."

Again, when Morgan pulled his car up at the curb outside the Center, he went around to open Barbara's door and offered his hand to help her out. The sidewalks were empty of pedestrians and a warm breeze stirred the air, ruffling Barbara's hair and carrying a faint scent of hamburgers and chilidogs from the fast-food restaurant at the center. Barbara hesitated a moment before saying good-bye.

"Thank you for lunch," she said sincerely, searching for something to say to express her feeling that they had shared so much more than lunch. But there weren't any appropriate words that wouldn't have seemed too presumptuous.

"Until Thursday, then," Morgan said with a warm smile.

"Thursday," Barbara repeated. He turned and took a

step away, but immediately turned back and swept Barbara into his arms. She was too surprised to resist; his kiss was sudden but not violent, his grip strong but not crushing. He pulled her off balance, so that her weight rested in his arms and she gripped his shoulders for support. Only the briefest, "Oh!" escaped her lips before his mouth covered hers and any protest she might have had was lost in the wonderful sensations he aroused in her. For a long wonderful moment, Barbara had no idea where she was or what was happening. But then the spell was broken when a group of children spilled out of the door of the Center, laughing, giggling, and yelling as they surrounded Morgan and Barbara. He set her back on her feet and looked around at his audience with an expression of good-natured embarrassment. Barbara felt a flush on her cheeks and looked over to see Brad leaning against the front of the building with an expression of strong disapproval on his face.

"My God!" Morgan muttered under his breath. "I don't think I would have ambushed you if I'd known the cavalry was just over the hill."

Barbara took a deep breath and recomposed her smile. "See you Thursday," she said quickly. As Morgan made his way back to his car through the crowd of children, Barbara watched him and then turned to face Brad. He chose to ignore her.

"All right. Now that we're outside, let's see your balloons," he said to the children. Each child raised a hand, grasping an imaginary balloon string. Brad had an almost hypnotic effect on the children. When he spoke, their attention turned completely to him, so Barbara and her embarrassing performance were instantly forgotten by them. "Good. Now your balloon is getting bigger and bigger and it's going to pull you up into the sky," he said, demonstrating with his own imaginary balloon. He raised his arm slowly, then grasped the "string" with his other hand and went up on his tiptoes. His motion was so fluid that one might almost believe he was actually being drawn up by an invisible balloon. The children followed suit.

Barbara had seen this exercise before. Brad used it to loosen up new groups of children. The pantomime routine was always played on the sidewalk, where the children could be seen by anyone passing by. The game of pretend, combined with the "public" performance, did wonders to ease the children's fears of looking silly in a dance class. A little girl with dark braids handed Barbara the string of her imaginary balloon and Barbara went along with the game, allowing the balloon to drag her arm into the air until she was standing on tiptoe. Then, with mock difficulty she hauled the balloon down and pretended to tie it to a parking meter. The children giggled at her performance.

"All right, everybody, back inside!" Brad called to the children, reserving a poisonous glance for Barbara. "When I come in there I want to see snakes crawling all over the floor!" The children all scrambled to get through the door first. "So, what was that?" he asked Barbara with a strong tone of disapproval in his voice.

"That was embarrassing," Barbara said evasively. "Did you really have to send the children out to rescue me?"

"I did nothing of the sort. Innocent that I am, I sent them out without checking first to see if there was anybody out here putting on a public show," he said darkly. "I suppose I should consider the sidewalks X-rated from now on?"

Barbara's temper rose to meet Brad's sarcasm. "Give me a break. That wasn't exactly Sodom and Gomorrah they got a peak at, Brad. I'm sure these children have seen a man and woman kiss before."

"No doubt," Brad said sourly. "But, the birds and bees aside, who was that? He looked familiar."

Barbara calmed down and let Brad's disapproval roll off her back. There was no reason to get upset every time Brad said something sarcastic; that was just his way. "He probably did look familiar, if you ever watch the news. That was the one and only Morgan Newman, of city council fame," Barbara replied with a wide smile.

"There goes the neighborhood," Brad said bitterly.

"What is your problem?" Barbara laughed. "You ought to be delighted. He's already helped us. You can expect a call from the people at 'Good Morning Windy City' any day now. At his suggestion, they're going to do a segment on the Center."

"Well, all I can say is, get what you can out of him," Brad replied.

"What do you mean by that?" Barbara asked, becoming annoyed once more with Brad's attitude.

"I mean, if you're going to run around with that type of dude, you'd better keep a tight hand on your purse and count the silverware after you eat."

"What *has* gotten into you today? Morgan Newman happens to be one of the nicest, most caring individuals I've ever met," she said defensively.

Brad raised an eyebrow. "I believe I just saw an example of that 'caring.' Just how long have you known this paragon of humanity?"

"Since last night, but that's beside the point."

"Is it?"

"Well, you don't know him at all, so who are you to talk?"

"I know enough. The man is a brass-plated phony.

I've lived in Chicago a lot longer than you have, Barbara. Chicago politicians have a flavor all their own."

"That's not fair! You're making a generalization based on rumor and innuendo. Not every politician is a crook—even in Chicago."

"I'd like to know how you can work in a sewer without getting any you-know-what on you."

Barbara shook her head. "You know what your problem is? You always believe the worst until proven otherwise. You walked into my office in New York less than three months ago, believing I was going to throw your proposal in the wastebasket—and look what really happened. You need to realize that people are basically good. That's what makes the bad ones stand out so much."

"You need to put aside those rose-colored glasses and see what's really going on in the world. The number of people who are actually willing to do anything for anybody else without getting something in return, is hardly worth counting. For every Mother Theresa, there are about fifty thousand muggers, rapists, and murderers."

"Then why bother, Brad?" Barbara retorted angrily. "All those kids in there are going to grow up to be muggers, rapists, and murderers. Why not just kick them into the street and let them get an early start?"

"Mr. Allen," a plaintive young voice called from inside the building. "Robert says he's a king cobra and he's going to bite everybody and we're all going to die!"

Brad stepped inside to face the little girl. "Well, you can go be a mongoose then," he said.

"What's a mongoose?"

"It's a small, furry animal, built low to the ground, that eats cobras," Brad explained in dramatic tones.

"How do mongooses go?" the girl asked with growing interest.

Brad crouched down on all fours in a surprisingly mongoose-like position and made several quick springs back and forth, clicking his tongue for sound effects. Barbara watched him for a moment, then went to her office at the back of the Center. The conversation was over for all practical purposes. Brad was absorbed in the children again, and that seemed to be the best thing for him. He saw the world as a threatening, perilous place. Only the children were exempted from that view.

"Well, never mind," she told herself. She didn't need Brad's approval, even though he was her closest friend in this city and she would have liked to have had it. But she was sure that Brad would come around in his own time.

As Barbara sifted through the papers on her desk, her mind kept skipping forward to Thursday night. The prospect of attending a charity fund raiser had never looked so attractive, and she had been to more benefits than she cared to count. No matter the cause, they generally boiled down to about the same routine. There would be a cocktail hour, a mediocre dinner, and then several people would make boring speeches. Afterwards the evening would continue with dancing to the music of an undistinguished band. Barbara smiled to herself as she thought about it. Everything would be so much simpler if people would just send in their money and spend an evening at home with their families.

Of course, this benefit was going to have one element that would raise it above all the rest. Morgan Newman was going to be her escort and the prospect of being with him gave her an unaccustomed thrill. Their lunch had convinced her that they had a great deal in common, and Barbara sensed that he held a potential for a warm and satisfying friendship. That had been what she had wanted to say on the sidewalk the moment before he kissed her. But that kiss had added an extra dimension and she could still feel the wonderful, warm pressure of his lips on her own. It had been so spontaneous, an indication that Morgan Newman was an unpredictable man. Certainly a city councilman knew enough to watch his behavior on a public street, but, in spite of that, he had taken a chance and given her a completely irresponsible kiss. It showed that there were dimensions of Morgan Newman that had nothing to do with the public man. He had revealed a side of himself that Barbara was sure he usually kept hidden underneath the responsible public figure he presented to the media.

"Thursday," Barbara murmured, wondering how she was going to wait two whole days.

# Chapter Four

"Stop that!" Barbara exclaimed as Bogey tugged the hem of her dress where it hung over the edge of the bed. "Pulling my dress onto the floor isn't going to stop me from going out, you devil."

Bogey dived under the bed as she took a swat at him to get him away from the dress, then his little black nose peaked out tentatively as he checked to see if the coast was clear.

"All right, you can come out, but behave yourself," she laughed. Turning back to the mirror, she continued to work on her hair, curling back her bangs and fluffing them with the brush, then spraying them lightly with hairspray to keep them in place. Barbara worked as quickly as she could. Morgan would be coming to pick her up any minute now, and she wasn't nearly ready. It seemed as if circumstances were conspiring to keep her from being on time. She hated to keep a man waiting while she finished dressing, it was so . . . female. But extra work at the Center had kept her occupied long past the time she had planned to leave, and Bogey wasn't helping. He never did. The little dog seemed to have a special sense of when she was dressing to go out and leave him alone for the evening, and he always managed to be just enough of a nuisance to make it very clear that he didn't like the idea.

As Barbara got the last curl in place, her doorbell rang. She let out a small frustrated sigh and put on her bathrobe to answer the door, hoping it wasn't Morgan. She still hadn't applied her makeup and had only gotten as far as putting on her half-slip and bra. Her worst fears were confirmed as she opened the door to Morgan.

If it were possible, he looked more impressive than he had on television. A tuxedo looked as natural on him as his casual sport jacket had, hugging his broad shoulders and fitting smoothly at his trim waist and narrow hips. His black bow tie was expertly tied and he was carrying a clear plastic flower box containing a white orchid corsage.

"Am I early?" he said with a bland smile.

"No, I'm late. I'm sorry. I'll be right with you. Have a seat," Barbara said in a single staccato explosion of words.

Morgan laughed. "Relax. We've got plenty of time. I'm the guest speaker, so they won't start without me. At the rate you're going, you're going to blow a gasket."

Barbara took a deep breath and forced herself to relax. "I'm really sorry," she said in a calmer tone. "I hate to keep anyone waiting. I got held up at work. Can I get you a glass of sherry while you're waiting?"

"No, I'm fine. You go and take your time to get ready. I'll just amuse myself by wandering around your living room, discovering all the deep dark secrets of your life."

"Is that supposed to make me relax?" Barbara laughed.

"It's supposed to make you hurry, in a relaxed and calm manner," Morgan replied with that special twinkle in his eye.

Back in her bedroom, Barbara scooped up Bogey and put him out into the living room with Morgan. "See if you can keep him in line," she said as she closed the door.

"You don't have to set the dog on me!" Morgan called out to her.

"I was talking to you," Barbara called back. "You keep him in line. He's being a real nuisance tonight."

"He just misses you when you go out. That's easy enough to understand."

Barbara sat down at her vanity and began to apply her makeup. After a few moments she heard strains of music coming from her stereo in the living room. Morgan had put on a recording of Bach's *The Well-Tempered Clavier.*

"I've already discovered several of your secrets," Morgan said through the closed door. "First, you have excellent taste in your decor. I'm sure this apartment has never been graced with a genuine Oriental rug, and a Matisse print on the wall among other things. Second, you like Baroque chamber music—very admirable."

Barbara leaned close to the mirror and combed mascara onto her eyelashes, enjoying a warm flush of pleasure at Morgan's approval of her taste. When she had moved into this old apartment building, the landlord and other tenants had raised their eyebrows considerably at her belongings as the movers had brought them up the stairs. At first she had despaired of making the dingy apartment comfortable and homey, but once the walls had been thoroughly scrubbed and her belongings put in place, she had become deeply satisfied with her new home. As much as she liked her apartment, however, it felt even better to know that Morgan liked it.

"And I'm discovering one of your secrets," she replied. "You're a shameless flatterer."

Morgan laughed. "Is it flattery if it's all the truth?"

"Don't talk to me," Barbara laughed. "You're just slowing me down."

She finished her makeup and stood to pull on her dress. The red silk crepe settled snugly around the swell of her breasts and her well-defined waist. The bodice featured a single built-up shoulder with a softly-pleated capelet sleeve that fell from it gracefully, and a matching set of pleats adorned the waistline on the opposite side, balancing the single sleeve and partially hiding the deep slit that allowed her to walk easily in the narrow skirt. The skirt itself flowed around her legs like crimson water, clinging to her graceful curves and swinging free around her ankles. The dress had an air of elegant simplicity despite its flamboyant color, and to complete the outfit, Barbara slipped on a pair of red silk high-heeled sandals. Nearly ready, she took a pair of gold earrings and a simple gold necklace from her jewelry box. She went out to the living room to join Morgan with the necklace in her hand.

"Would you fasten this for me?" she asked, hanging the necklace in place and holding the free ends behind her neck.

Morgan came up behind her to take the clasp and deftly fasten it. "A delightful chore," he said quietly. She felt his warm breath on the back of her neck and an involuntary shiver went down her spine. "The color of your dress agrees with you. It brings out the radiance of your beautiful red hair." As he let go of the necklace, his fingers traced the slope of her bare shoulder, sending a thrill of pleasure through her body. "You're going to put every woman in the room to shame," he murmured in her ear as his arms circled her waist and drew her close to him.

"We're keeping a lot of people waiting," Barbara reminded him softly as she pulled away. The spell woven by his strong arms and delicate touch was difficult to break, but something told Barbara that it was up to her to keep things moving right now. The tone of Morgan's voice intimated that he was in no hurry to get to the Clean Up Our Parks benefit.

"Responsibility . . ." Morgan said in a bemused voice. "You know, there are moments when I'd like to chuck it all and please myself for a change." His eyes lingered on Barbara's face and a slow smile spread across his lips. "But then again, I wouldn't want to miss the reactions when everyone sees the beautiful woman I'm escorting tonight."

Barbara picked up her clutch purse but Morgan motioned for her to wait. "I've still got two more things to put on you. This is the first one," he said, removing the corsage from its box. "I didn't know what color you were wearing, so I thought white would be the safest choice." He expertly pinned the flower to the shoulder of her dress. "And this is the second," he whispered as his lips descended to hers. The kiss was a brief, gentle contact, yet Barbara's heart beat faster just the same. Her resolve to leave the apartment and go on to the banquet weakened for a moment, but Morgan pulled away and opened the door for her. "I'd like to do a much better job of that, but I'd hate for you to have to go back and put your makeup on again," he said as they left the apartment and Barbara locked the door behind them.

The cocktail hour was well underway by the time they arrived at the benefit. The hall was decorated to resemble a park, with benches placed around the edges of the room, potted bushes strategically located to screen different areas, a fountain splashing away in the center of the room and a huge papier mâché tree spreading over the speakers' table. A wooden gazebo had been constructed at one end of the dance floor for the band. The room was crowded with couples holding drinks in one hand and little plates of hors d'oeuvres in the other. Barbara had a sudden feeling of déjà vu as she hesitated in the doorway. The theme of the decorations might be different, but, in essence, she had been to this party many times before.

A short man with wavy blond hair and a practically invisible blond mustache met them at the door and pumped Morgan's hand. "I'm glad you could make it, Morgan," he said with relief.

"This is Tom Staley, chairman of the Parks Committee," Morgan said, presenting the young man to Barbara. "Tom, this is my friend, Barbara Danbury. She's the administrator of the Thirty-seventh Street Center for the Performing Arts."

Tom Staley smiled first with recognition, then with a frank appreciation of Barbara's appearance. "Ah, I've heard of that. Isn't that the dance school run by Bret Allen?"

"Brad Allen," Barbara corrected. "Yes. But we have programs in drama and instrumental music as well."

"I've heard people talking," Tom went on. "I understand you've been doing some fantastic things there, but I had no idea that the administrator of the project was so charming," he said with a gallant flourish. "I'm going to corner you later on and run an idea I've got past you. But for now, would you like a drink?"

"No thank you," Barbara said with a smile.

"Well, I'll talk to you later," Tom said. "I hope you enjoy the dinner." He started to greet another couple coming through the door, and Morgan guided Barbara into the crowd with a gentle hand on her elbow.

Once they were in the midst of the gathering, Barbara found it hard to keep track of Morgan. He circulated from group to group, greeting people he knew and introducing himself to others. In the beginning, as they moved from group to group, Morgan always began by introducing Barbara and explaining her connection with the Thirty-seventh Street Center. To her surprise, everybody seemed to have heard of it. Only days earlier she had despaired of getting any publicity for her project, but now it seemed that everybody in town knew what she was doing. Somewhere in the third or fourth group of people someone asked her to elaborate on her programs, and before she knew what happened, Morgan had been swept away by a man who insisted he had something very important to talk about. After that, Barbara found herself circulating on her own, though she was far from isolated in the crowd of strangers. Enough people had seen her come in with Morgan that she was constantly besieged by people approaching her to find out more about her and her relationship to Morgan.

She was relieved when it was time to be seated for the dinner and she could take her place at the speakers' table between Morgan and Tom Staley. Morgan pulled out her chair and seated her gallantly. As he slid her chair in, he bent over and spoke quietly in her ear.

"Sorry about that," he apologized. "I didn't mean to lose you that way."

"That's all right," Barbara replied with a smile. "I know how to handle myself at this kind of affair."

"That's what worries me," Morgan chuckled. "If I leave you alone too long, you'll find someone who has time for you and I'll be left out in the cold."

"Beware," Barbara whispered impishly. "At the end of an evening, I just might ignore the man who was ignoring me at the beginning."

Morgan's face contorted into an expression of mock pain as he seated himself next to her.

The meal was better than average for an affair of this type. The chicken Kiev was slightly overcooked and the broccoli was limp, but the dinner began with an excellent fruit salad, and dessert was a refreshing surprise. Following the park theme of the banquet, an ice cream cart traveled among the diners, handing out cones in a choice of several flavors, and Barbara had to give the banquet planners extra points for the unusual idea.

Since the head table was served first, most of the people seated there finished their meals before the rest of the room. Barbara looked over to Morgan, but found him absorbed in conversation with the elderly woman seated on his other side. Looking to Tom Staley on her other side, she found him just finishing his meal.

"You said you had something you wanted to tell me about?" she asked politely, to start the conversation.

"Yes, I have an idea," he replied enthusiastically. "Tell me what you think of this. Part of the Parks Committee's goal is to get more people out to use the parks. A lot of people are driving out of the city these days to go to a park, because our own parks have gotten a bad image. They were dirty, sometimes dangerous, and not always pleasant. We're out to change all that, and we've already done a lot toward cleaning up—the money we're raising here tonight is going to do more in that direction. And with Councilman Newman's support, we've managed to get increased police patrols to help deal with the crime problem. Now, the largest part of our remaining job is to draw the right kind of people back to the parks. To do that, I'd like to start an annual festival of the performing arts. We don't have the funds to bring in a lot of big-name performers, but everybody loves to watch talented kids, and I understand that's your specialty."

Barbara smiled as she considered the idea. "You want the Thirty-seventh Street Center to put on a series of recitals in the parks," she said thoughtfully. "It sounds like a good idea, but you have to understand that we're just getting started. We don't have many advanced students yet. I'll talk to Brad. It would take us several weeks to put something together . . ."

"Well, why don't I call you at the Center sometime next week and we can discuss the details? We can bring Mr. Allen in on it then. But I'm really excited about the idea. I think it has real potential."

"Let me ask you something," Barbara said. "How did you hear about the Center? Until just recently, we haven't had too much publicity."

"Why, everybody is talking about it," Tom replied with a puzzled expression. "You'll have to excuse me now, I've got to get up and do my chairman thing." The guests were finished with their meals, and it was time to begin the program.

Tom approached the podium and tapped on a nearby water glass to get the attention of the audience. "Ladies and gentlemen, now that we have all enjoyed a delicious dinner, we have a special pleasure in store. With us tonight is one of the most distinguished and dynamic councilmen in our fair city. This man's accomplishments speak for themselves. In two years on the Chicago City Council, he has been the principle proponent of more 'pro-people' legislation than any councilman in recent memory. And for the Parks Committee, he has been a special guardian angel. Not only has he arranged for matching city funds for our clean-up efforts, but his influence with the police department has provided us with the extra park patrols that have resulted in a substantial reduction in park crime. I'm sure that you all realize that our guest speaker needs no introduction, so I will surrender the floor to Morgan Newman."

There was a polite round of applause while Morgan took the podium. He stood with a relaxed, confident air and waited patiently until the room quieted. "Thank you, Tom," he said with a smile. "Actually, after that excellent meal, I think I'd rather crawl off somewhere and take a nap rather than talk, but since I said I'd give a speech—and I am a politician and we're expected to do such things—I guess I'll find a few words to say." There was a brief pause while the audience chuckled appreciatively.

"While I was sitting here listening to Tom introduce me, I was feeling a little bit embarrassed," Morgan continued. "He kept talking about all the wonderful things I've done for the Parks Committee, and I came here tonight planning to thank the Parks Committee for all the wonderful things they've done for me—and for every other resident of this city. A city is like a living creature. The buildings and the streets are the skeleton and the people are the blood that flows through the veins. We in the government are like the nervous system. But the heart of any city lies in its parks. A city that lets its parks die is letting its heart and soul die. And no matter how prosperous and economically stable a city is, without that heart it's nothing but a lot of tall buildings and harried people . . ."

Barbara listened to Morgan's speech with a feeling of admiration. His speaking style combined a relaxed, intimate tone with a storyteller's knack for spinning images. He held the audience in thrall. Yet, when she tried to analyze what he was saying, she realized that he was actually saying very little. He praised the Parks Committee's work and pledged support for vague things like the quality of life and the survival of the special flavor of the city. But he gave no assurances that the special funding he had arranged would continue past the current budget.

The audience applauded enthusiastically as Morgan surrendered the podium to Tom Staley and took his seat next to Barbara. Tom introduced the next speaker, an elderly woman who was the president of the Windy City Garden Club and was speaking to pledge her club's help with the landscaping in the parks. Her voice carried an elderly tremor and her speech was slightly confused, but the diners listened politely enough. Barbara focused her attention on Morgan, who, to her surprise, was giving the speaker his rapt attention. As the older woman continued with her speech, she would glance down occasionally at Morgan seated beside her and would instantly brighten her expression and tone of voice. Barbara got the strong impression that the speaker was relying on Morgan for some sort of moral support to get through her speech. When she finally finished, there was a polite patter of applause.

The remainder of the program consisted of Tom Staley handing out awards to people who had made outstanding contributions to the Parks Committee. With the formal business concluded, the band started to set up in the gazebo and the diners began to drift away from the tables. For what seemed like the first time in hours, Morgan turned his attention to Barbara and stood to help her from her seat.

"I hope you've saved the first dance for me," he said with a smile.

"Why of course," Barbara replied. "It may be my only chance to talk to you all evening."

Morgan's face held an expression of sincere contrition. "I'm really sorry. I know I've been neglecting you."

"That's all right," Barbara said. "Believe it or not, I understand that you're here to work. Bringing a date is a mere social formality. I knew exactly what I was getting into when I agreed to come tonight."

Morgan's arm slid around her waist as he guided her toward the dance floor. "I wouldn't be too quick to be so understanding," Morgan chuckled. "You're giving up your advantage. This may be your only chance to have me at your mercy."

As the band struck up its first strains, Barbara and Morgan were the first couple to take the floor. He led with confident grace, guiding Barbara in a sweeping arc to the rhythm of the Strauss waltz. Only a few couples joined them, and Barbara had the strong feeling that she and Morgan were the center of attention for most of the people at the benefit. As they swirled and turned through the music, every face that Barbara saw on the sides of the dance floor had eyes squarely turned in their direction. She momentarily felt as if she had stepped into a Fred Astaire movie, assuming the role of Ginger Rogers.

"I don't really think I have you at my mercy," Barbara said humorously as they danced. "You seem to have the situation firmly under control."

"But do I?" Morgan said innocently. "I keep remembering what you said about no woman going out with me a second time. I'd hate to think that next time I call you, you're going to turn me down."

Barbara laughed. "You're always working an angle, aren't you? All the time you're apologizing for neglecting me, you're counting on how grateful I'm going to be for all the publicity you've arranged for the Center."

"Publicity? Me?" Morgan said with mock innocence. "What do you mean?"

"I mean that two days ago nobody had heard of the Thirty-seventh Street Center. Tonight, everyone I've met has heard of it. Not only that, I'm informed that absolutely everybody is talking about it. Now, putting together what I know about you and your methods, I'm guessing that 'absolutely everybody' really means that Morgan Newman has been talking about it."

Morgan laughed. "And I thought I was being subtle. You see right through me. I suppose my efforts have all been in vain."

"It depends on what you're trying to accomplish," Barbara said with a cryptic smile. "If you think that publicizing the Center will make me fall hopelessly in love with you, guess again. On the other hand, if you're demonstrating your capacity for loyal friendship, you're definitely scoring points."

"And what would it take to make you fall hopelessly in love with me?" Morgan asked with a glint in his eye.

Barbara chuckled. "I'll never tell. I don't intend to give up all my advantages."

"In that case, I'll just have to keep trying," Morgan replied as he hugged her closer. "Maybe later on I can trade in some of those 'loyal friend' points for 'hopelessly in love' points. By the way, what did you think of my speech?"

Barbara hesitated for a few beats of the music before she answered. "It was very . . . political," she responded slowly.

Morgan winced. "Shot down again," he said humorously. "You aren't doing anything for my ego tonight, Barbara."

"Your ego doesn't need any help. But honestly, I didn't mean that as an insult," Barbara said sincerely. "It was a very good speech. I was really caught up in it at first. It was only when I started thinking about it that I realized you weren't promising anything you couldn't deliver."

Morgan smiled. "You have a sharp facility for logical analysis," he said. "It's fortunate for politicians in general that not too many people share your talent. There are several approaches to a speech of this kind. One is to lie and tell the people exactly what they want to hear. If you can't deliver at a later date—make excuses and say you tried your best. The second is to get up and tell the simple truth. It's very honest, and in some situations simple honesty will gain a lot of support. But at a dinner of this kind, people don't really want to hear complete honesty. They're here to congratulate themselves for the good job they've been doing and they want to believe that everything is going to be great in the future. I don't like lying, but very little would be served by disappointing these people with the unfortunate truth about next year's budget. So I opted for system three—speak in vaguely glowing terms about intangible concepts."

Barbara's face took on a look of concern. "Then these people are going to be disappointed? They aren't going to get any funds next year?"

"I didn't say that. I don't have a crystal ball and I can only cast one vote in the council. But austerity is a fact of life in city government these days. I intend to support the parks' funding, but not at the expense of more important programs like maintaining the mass transit system or preventing layoffs in the city administration."

The music ended, but Morgan made no attempt to leave the dance floor. Barbara stood by his side, slightly troubled by what he had just said.

"I'm going to make a new rule," Morgan said with a warm smile. "I'm not going to talk politics with you anymore. It makes you frown and I like your face so much better when you're smiling."

"I didn't mean to look as if I disapproved," Barbara replied. "It just seems a shame for all these people to think that everything is going to be fine when there's so much uncertainty."

"There's uncertainty in everything," Morgan replied wisely. "Who knows how things are going to turn out? For example, what certainty do I have that you're going to agree to come up to my place tonight for a drink after we leave here?"

Barbara found herself laughing again. "Well, I don't have a crystal ball," she teased. "I guess we'll just have to wait and see."

Just then the band started playing a Glenn Miller arrangement of "Stardust," and Morgan swept Barbara back into his arms. A few more couples joined them on the dance floor and, feeling less like she was on display, Barbara let the music and Morgan's compelling magnetism carry her along.

She had always loved dancing, but partners who were both tall enough and truly good dancers had always been difficult to find. It suddenly struck her that she hadn't once been aware of her height since she had started to dance with Morgan. It wasn't just that he was tall, it was also the way he moved. His step was so sure and confident that there was no room for Barbara to feel any kind of awkwardness. His lead was so easy to follow that she found herself moving along with him as if they had been dancing together for years.

They danced through song after song, never leaving the floor while other couples came and went. Barbara began to forget about the benefit and the other guests, feeling as if she and Morgan were alone with their own private orchestra. She had his complete attention, and as they talked and moved to the gentle rhythms of the music, it seemed that nothing could distract him from the single purpose of being her partner. Then, as the band took its first break, Morgan glanced at his watch.

"Would you mind if we left now?" he asked.

Barbara was surprised at the suggestion, but more than willing to acquiesce. Fatigue from her long day was beginning to catch up with her, however much she was enjoying her time with Morgan. "Not at all," she replied with a smile.

"That invitation for a drink at my place is still open," he said with a smile.

"Is that why you're in such a hurry to leave?" Barbara laughed. "Are you that anxious to get me alone?"

"Partly," Morgan replied. "But, in the interest of honesty, I also want to leave because it's ten-thirty."

Barbara looked puzzled. "Do you turn into a pumpkin at eleven?"

Morgan laughed out loud. "Not exactly. We had an important vote in the council today and I've been ducking reporters all afternoon. They knew I was coming here tonight, so I'm willing to bet that there's a group of them waiting outside. If we leave now, they'll just have time to get back to their stations for the eleven o'clock news."

Barbara shook her head, trying to figure out what

Morgan was up to. "But why didn't you just talk to them this afternoon?"

"Because most of the other councilmen did. They each got to give about fifteen seconds worth of reaction on the six o'clock news. By making them pursue me, I get the eleven o'clock news all to myself."

"Are you sure you want to tell me all this?" Barbara asked in wonderment. "Aren't you afraid you'll spoil your ethical and honest image?"

"I think it's only fair to warn you that we're going to walk out of here into a crowd of television reporters," he replied. "As for my image, I hope you're interested in getting to know more than my image."

Barbara took a deep breath. "Well, forewarned is forearmed," she said. "I may need that drink after all. . . ."

Morgan took Barbara's arm and they strolled out into the night. His prediction proved correct. A knot of television cameramen and reporters was waiting on the sidewalk outside the hall. As Barbara and Morgan came down the walk, bright portable lights flashed on and Barbara was temporarily blinded. She held tightly to Morgan's arm for guidance. The reporters crowded around and half a dozen microphones were shoved unceremoniously under Morgan's nose. He paused and waited for the questions.

The interview went much as the one Barbara had viewed in the hospital. Morgan answered questions and made jokes with the reporters, as if being surrounded by television cameras was the most natural thing in the world to him. The only difference this time was that Barbara was a part of the activity. She found the cameras and lights unnerving and wondered at Morgan's calm, relaxed manner. She felt strangely invisible standing next to him, for though she knew she was as much in the picture as he was, everybody's attention was focused exclusively on him.

Afterward, she wasn't completely sure what the press conference had been about. It had something to do with the police, but Barbara's attention was drawn to Morgan himself more than what he was saying. In the paralyzing light of the television cameras, her only grasp on her composure seemed to come from Morgan; he was a calm pillar she could hang onto to weather the storm. She grasped his arm and focused her eyes on his strong, calm face as he deftly fielded various questions. The reporters were as agitated as Morgan was calm, all trying to get their own questions in next by shouting and waving their microphones each time Morgan finished a reply.

He accommodated them gracefully for several minutes, but then, as their questions began to repeat themselves, he suddenly cut them off short. "Thank you, that will be all," he said with a tone of finality. He put an arm around Barbara's waist and propelled her forward through the crowd. The reporters parted to make way, then closed in behind to follow them to the car, still trying to get in one more question before Morgan left. But he had decided to conclude the interview and made no more responses, no matter how insistent they were. As the car pulled out of the parking lot, lights followed and one particularly insistent reporter tapped on Morgan's window, trying to get him to answer one more question.

Barbara sat back in her seat and let out a sigh of relief as Morgan drove away, leaving the media people behind. "How do you stay so calm when everybody is yelling for your attention?" she asked as he merged onto the freeway.

"It's something you have to get used to," he said with

a smile. "They seem like sharks in a feeding frenzy at first, but after you've been around them for a while, you get to know them as individuals and realize that they act like that because they're all under pressure to bring back an earth-shaking story. They're not really that bad; they're doing their job, just like I am."

# Chapter Five

Morgan handed Barbara a crystal goblet of pale white wine as he guided her out to the balcony of his apartment, overlooking the city. In many ways, his apartment was vaguely like his office, especially with its panoramic view of the Chicago skyline. From this vantage, Barbara could look northwest, out over the dark water of Lake Michigan that was sprinkled with the lights of ships. To the northeast, the skyline of the city sparkled in all its nighttime glory. The headlights of cars crawled along in the distant streets, like earthbound lightning bugs. Bright neon signs crowned many of the taller downtown buildings, and random patterns of glowing windows defined the shapes of the skyscrapers and lesser buildings.

The bright patterns of light that made up the city rivaled, but didn't defeat, the canopy of stars overhead. A cool breeze drifted in from the lake, carrying its subtle fragrance. Barbara looked over the panorama laid out below, above, and before her and imagined herself flying over the city—as invisible as the breeze that was ruffling her hair.

Morgan leaned against the planter that formed the balcony railing and looked into Barbara's face. "Like the view?" he asked languidly as he took her free hand in his.

"I was thinking about a Dr. Suess story," Barbara replied, feeling somewhat embarrassed to admit it. "Yurtle the Turtle."

Morgan laughed. "Now, why does that seem like a non sequitur?"

"Yurtle the Turtle was king of everything he could see," Barbara explained. "So he kept climbing up higher to see more."

"I'm not sure how I should take that."

"It doesn't mean anything," Barbara said, turning to face Morgan. "It just came to mind because of the beautiful view. You have your castle on a mountaintop so you can look down on your kingdom." Barbara took a sip of her wine and smiled at him.

Morgan seemed momentarily chagrined and turned away to look out over the city. "What happened?" he asked quietly.

"What?"

"To Yurtle the Turtle."

Barbara chuckled. "He climbed up too high and fell back down into the swamp. After that, he was just king of the mud."

Morgan was strangely silent as he looked out into the night.

"Don't take it too seriously," Barbara said, stepping closer to Morgan and squeezing his hand to win back his attention. "It's not a prophecy—just a kids' story."

Morgan turned to face Barbara, an odd smile on his face. "I don't know why I want to hang around with

you," he said in a voice that was only partly humorous.
"You always see right through me. Tell me, Barbara
Danbury, do you read minds?"

"Only after they come out in paperback," Barbara
said with a twinkle in her eye.

"Why aren't you married?" he asked abruptly. Barbara was surprised by the transition, but fielded the
question smoothly.

"When I was nineteen, I couldn't find a young man
who met my specifications. When I was twenty-five, I
wanted to concentrate on my career and I didn't feel I
could afford the extra burdens of a husband and children until I had established myself. I'm well established
now, but I have to admit that I'm still in no hurry to get
married. I guess the truth is that I like my life the way it
is. Why aren't you married? It would certainly be an
advantage in your line of work."

Morgan hesitated before he replied. "When I was
twenty-five, I was a civil liberties lawyer working about
eighteen hours a day, and I didn't think it would be fair
to ask any woman to share that kind of a life. After I
went into politics everybody kept telling me that I
ought to get married, but I couldn't see doing it for
purely political reasons. I guess, like you, I'm used to
having my life the way it is. Actually, I think the mys-
tique of being the bachelor councilman has been almost
as much of a political advantage as a well-trained wife
would have been."

"One more thing we have in common," Barbara said.
"We're both confirmed bachelors."

"Do you have a boyfriend? Back in New York, I
mean."

"I have male friends," Barbara responded vaguely,
"no one particularly special. I won't bother bouncing

that question back at you—your love life is a matter of public record."

"Not as much as you think," Morgan replied with a smile. "One of the most important skills of working with the press is only letting them know what you *want* them to know."

Barbara let her attention drift back to the twinkling cityscape. The dark sky and the bright lights had a soothing effect on her, and the cool night air felt good on her face. She was enjoying this feeling of closeness with Morgan as he stood beside her looking out over the city.

"Do you miss New York?" Morgan asked gently.

"Not really. New York is a very special place, there isn't another city like it in the world, but little by little Chicago seems to be getting under my skin. Last Saturday I rode the El downtown and went to the Museum of Science and Industry—just like a tourist. Isn't that silly? But I've been hearing all the kids at the Center talk about it and I started to feel like I was really missing something. I enjoyed myself."

"I've lived here all my life and I've never been to most of the museums," Morgan replied. "One of these Saturday afternoons we'll have to go see the Museum of Natural History together." Morgan turned to face Barbara and placed his warm hands on her shoulders, pulling her closer to him. She looked directly into his eyes, only to see that he was looking intently into her own face, as if searching for something. For a moment, Barbara thought she saw a weariness in his eyes that wasn't reflected in his relaxed posture or his friendly banter.

When their lips met, if wasn't as if either of them had consciously moved. It was more like a flowing together—like two drops of water on a windowpane combining to become one larger drop. Morgan's arms

closed around Barbara, drawing her to the warmth of
his chest. She was vaguely aware of her arms, almost
under their own volition, rising to circle his neck and
for a long moment she let the wonderful feelings of
longing and satisfaction rise and swirl through her
body.

Then deep within her, in a place that seemed never to
have been touched before, a new longing was born. At
first it was only a reluctance to break away from
Morgan's strong embrace and trade the warmth of his
body for the cool night air. But it soon had more depth
and dimension than the mere touching of bodies. Under
the spell of this new feeling Barbara's point of view
changed subtly, and for the first time in her life she
wondered how she could go on living by herself. The
thought passed through her mind and was lost in the
rising storm of physical sensation almost instantly, but
now that she had been touched she knew she'd never be
the same again.

"Shall we go back inside?" Morgan's voice whispered very close to Barbara's ear. She nodded, and with
Morgan's arm protectively around her waist, they
slowly left the balcony. The lights inside were low and
Morgan left Barbara's side for a moment to put a tape
on. The precise, subdued strains of Pacobel's Canon in
D Major filled the room and Barbara smiled in recognition of the piece.

"I see I'm not the only person with a taste for Baroque
music," she said.

Morgan made no reply, but returned to Barbara and
took her hands in his own. She looked deep into his
eyes again and saw that they had changed. The weariness seemed to have passed and in its place was soft
glimmer, like moonlight on moving water. He seemed
younger and more resilient than he had a moment

A PUBLIC AFFAIR                    77

before, and Barbara wondered if she could ever get to know all the changing facets of this man. He had so many different faces and each one seemed to come from his heart. Barbara leaned forward ever so slightly and let her lips brush his.

"Maybe you shouldn't have come here tonight, Barbara," Morgan said softly.

"Why not?" Barbara asked in a puzzled tone.

"Because you're too beautiful to resist." He let go of one of her hands and brushed his fingertips over the white slope of Barbara's uncovered shoulder. A delightful shiver ran down her spine.

"Maybe I don't want you to resist," Barbara replied in a breathy voice. Morgan raised her hand to his lips and one by one kissed the tips of her fingers, sending tiny thrills of pleasure through her arm to her already pounding heart. Then, with her hand still firmly in his own, he led her from the living room into his bedroom.

The room fit perfectly with all the others she had seen Morgan in. The beige plush carpet formed a neutral background for several turquoise Oriental scatter rugs and a turquoise and brown bedspread. The furniture was modern, dark mahogany, and the overall effect was simple and uncluttered but extremely elegant.

"I think I should have put on Wagner instead of Pacobel," Morgan said in a bemused voice. "When I first discovered that you liked Baroque music I thought it was appropriate because you seemed like a Baroque composition—the perfection of style—but now I realize that's not right. With your beautiful, flaming red hair you are too much your own person for that. I look at the sure, graceful way you move your wonderful long body, and I can only believe I've come to know one of Richard Wagner's Valkyries."

Barbara blushed under his steady gaze. "I should

have known that you'd like Wagner," she said softly.
"He fits you perfectly, so full of force and strength . . ."

Morgan pulled Barbara close and kissed her eyelids
with a delicate touch that made her heart beat faster and
stirred the deep longing in her body. When his hands
slowly lowered the zipper on her dress, she let the soft
fabric fall to the floor around her feet with only the
slightest shrug of her shoulders. The soft material
became a limp red pile at her feet topped with the white
orchid Morgan had given her.

His fingers then traced the delicate angles of her bare
shoulders and dropped behind her to open the back of
her strapless bra. As the full, womanly swell of her
breasts was released, his free hand caressed her soft,
sensitive flesh and teased the rosy nipples into hard
peaks.

Barbara let out a sigh of pleasure as she leaned against
the solid support of Morgan's body, and the material of
his shirt felt smooth and crisp against her naked skin.
She wrapped her arms around his neck and pressed
herself against every contour of his body as his hands
found the supple curves of her back and moved in ever
lower swirls to her hips.

Barbara unclasped her hands behind Morgan's neck
and leaned away from him, just far enough to unfasten
his tie and the small mother-of-pearl buttons of his
shirt. Beneath, she found the smooth skin, hard
muscles, and curly brown hair of his chest. He moaned
softly and pulled her to him gently. Then, as bare skin
met bare skin, his lips found the sensitive hollow of her
neck and shoulders. A moment later, Barbara's half-slip
and panties followed her dress to the floor and she
stepped out of them to lie down on the bed while
Morgan removed the last of his own clothing.

Before joining her on the bed, Morgan paused to let

his eyes linger on the reclining length of her body. As he came to her, he placed his hand lightly on her cheek, then drew it slowly along her neck, down her chest to caress the flat expanse of her abdomen and circle the full, feminine swell of her hips. Barbara's body tensed and rose to greet his exciting touch. Waves of ecstasy coursed through her as his fingertips found the deliciously sensitive flesh of her thighs and swept down the length of her legs. Her eyes opened partially and she could see his powerful, masculine body above her.

Her chest rose and fell in the swelling rhythm of her desire as Morgan continued his ministrations. Then, when she felt she could wait no longer, her voice forced itself from her burning chest. "Now—come to me now," she said in a voice husky with desire.

He acknowledged her plea with the hard, masculine proof of his own yearning, and as he penetrated her, joining them together in the most intimate way, she experienced a satisfaction that exceeded anything she had ever felt. Her hips rose and fell to meet the rhythm of his passion, and together their hunger deepened to become an agonizing ecstasy that burst around them in a moment of blinding light that carried them to another reality. Her fingers dug into the sturdy muscles of his shoulders as every fiber of her body tensed and then exploded with the fulfillment of her deepest need.

Morgan's body relaxed and he let out a deep sigh of satisfaction. For a long, leisurely time they lay together, savoring the receding echoes of their lovemaking. Then Morgan turned over to cradle Barbara against him. Resting her head against his strong but yielding shoulder, she trailed her fingers over his warm chest and arms.

"My Viking princess," Morgan whispered languidly.

Barbara had to laugh softly at Morgan's words. He raised his head to give her a questioning look.

"I don't think I have a drop of Norse blood in me. I'm French and English," she explained.

Morgan chuckled in return. "I don't care. You have the soul of a Norse goddess."

Barbara's mouth curled in an impish smile. "Do you mean soul or legs? I'll bet you say that to every girl over five feet eight."

"I wouldn't want an inch less of you." He ran his fingers through her tousled curls and kissed her lightly on the forehead. "Do you have to be at work early tomorrow?"

"I'm the boss. I don't have to be at work until I feel like it," Barbara said lazily.

"Good. I don't have any appointments in the morning. We can sleep in." He yawned and let his eyes drift closed. Barbara savored the regular sound of his breathing until her own eyes closed in contented sleep.

The regular sound of Morgan's breathing was still in her ear and a subdued morning light filtered through the open-weave curtains when Barbara awoke. She sat up and carefully slipped off the edge of the bed so as not to disturb Morgan's sleep. She found a robe hanging on the inside of the bathroom door, and slipped it on as she went to the kitchen to fix herself a cup of coffee. A quick survey of the refrigerator revealed eggs, bacon, and orange juice, so on impulse Barbara set about preparing breakfast. When the eggs were nicely arranged on buttered toast and a pot of coffee was steaming on the stove, she went back to the bedroom to rouse Morgan. She found him half awake, delaying the moment of leaving the warm bed.

"Whatever you're doing out there smells delicious," he said sleepily. "There's another robe in the closet. Will you do me a favor and toss it over here?" He stood up and stretched like a big jungle cat, then put on the robe, tying it at his waist.

They took Barbara's culinary efforts onto the patio and enjoyed their meal in the bright morning sunshine. A light haze had settled close to the ground, making it seem even more distant than it was, but the tops of the buildings sparkled in the clear morning air.

"You have a way with eggs, *madame*," Morgan said with an appreciative smile.

"You should see what I can do when I really get going. I studied cooking in Paris at one time."

"Really?" Morgan asked with a raised eyebrow. "I think I'll have to keep you here to find out what else you can do."

Barbara chuckled. "I think one of the worst disadvantages to living by yourself is cooking. I love to cook, but I never have anyone to do it for. If I just ate it myself I'd weigh three hundred pounds."

"Why does a dedicated career woman like yourself go to cooking school in France?" Morgan asked in an interested tone.

"Uncle Horace never spoiled me, with one exception: I could have anything I asked for if it had to do with my education. I wanted to go to cooking school, so he decided to send me to the best. But that was a long time ago."

"Uncle Horace? Are you talking about Horace Calvin of Calvin Foundation fame? You're related to one of the wealthiest men this country has ever known?" Morgan asked in surprise.

"Not really related. My mother died when I was born and my father was Uncle Horace's lawyer. When my father died, Uncle Horace took me in. He was very close to Dad, and I didn't have any living relatives."

"Then you're not just an administrator for the Calvin

Foundation—you *are* the Calvin Foundation," Morgan said slowly.

"No. Believe me, I'm just an administrator. Financially, Uncle Horace left me relatively little," Barbara explained. "He felt very strongly about inheriting fortunes; being a self-made man, he believed that others should follow his example."

"Have I mentioned that you look positively ravishing in my bathrobe?" Morgan said, changing the subject with a charming smile.

Barbara laughed. "And can you imagine the sensation I'm going to cause when I go home this morning in my evening clothes?"

"In that case I'll just have to keep you here until tonight when your clothes become appropriate again," Morgan replied with a sparkle in his eye. He reached across the table and took her hand.

"If you do that, we'll end up going out to do the town again and coming back here again and I'll never get home," Barbara said.

"Are you in such a rush to get home?"

Barbara smiled hesitantly. Morgan seemed to be asking her for so much more than she had bargained for. "If I don't go home fairly soon, Bogey will call Goodwill to come after my furniture," she said humorously.

"Ah, Bogey! How could I have forgotten?" Morgan exclaimed, striking his forehead with the heel of his hand as if remembering the crux of the matter. "Never romance a woman with children if you want a moment of peace."

"What a shame," Barbara replied with a laugh, "he speaks so highly of you."

"I positively refuse to take you home before you tell me when you'll come back to fix dinner. I'm already hungry for some of that French cooking."

Barbara let out a mock sigh. "It's always the same, let them know you can cook and men are only interested in one thing. Did I go to Vassar to become a scullery maid?"

"You were born to be a queen," Morgan said warmly.

"And you were born to be a politician," she replied impishly. "Uncle Horace always warned me to beware of flatterers."

"There you go again, cutting me to the bone," he said in a tone that was half serious. "How can you bear to be seen with me—you a princess, and me shamelessly pursuing the only profession that Americans rate as less honest than selling used cars."

"Don't worry, I trust you," Barbara replied with a chuckle. "If only because I can see right through you."

"I do believe you can," Morgan said thoughtfully.

Barbara finally arrived at the Center a little before two o'clock. Brad was finishing up with his Junior Creative Movement class, and the halting sounds of a child practicing on the piano were coming from the music room. Brad gave her a withering glance as she crossed the studio area. Barbara ignored him and stopped to look over the group of five- to eight-year-olds who were following Brad through a set of simple modern dance movements.

She had been home to shower and change her clothes, donning a pair of black cotton jeans and a light blue chambray shirt for work. Her skin had taken on a special glow and there was an indescribable light in her eyes.

To her delight, as Barbara scanned the group of children she saw Ossie, her midget con man, in the middle of the class. He was concentrating on the stretching movement Brad was leading, but after a moment the boy noticed her and flashed his toothiest grin.

"All right, gang, that's it for today," Brad announced. "For Monday, I want everybody to go home and keep your eyes open. Find something that you see every day and make up a motion that will tell everybody what it is without actually saying the name."

The children started to scatter, and Ossie made a bee-line for Barbara. "Hey there, Miz D.," he said brightly. "I think your place is all right."

"Well, thank you," Barbara replied. "I'm glad you approve." As she spoke to Ossie, she kept an eye on Brad, whose face was more clouded than usual. He had something on his mind and Barbara was sure it had to do with her, though she didn't know what she could have done to offend him. Knowing that Brad wanted to talk to her, she stalled anyway, if only to delay the unpleasantness. She was still riding a wave of euphoria from her night with Morgan and didn't want to lose the feeling. "How's your grandmother, Ossie?" she asked pleasantly.

"She fine, 'cept her arthritis actin' up," Ossie said seriously, delighted to have an adult talk to him as an equal. "You sure look fine beside that Mr. Newman, Miz D."

Barbara was surprised. Ossie hadn't been in the group of children who had seen her with Morgan on the sidewalk in front of the Center, so what could he be talking about? "I'm glad you approve," she said carefully, "but when did you see me with Mr. Newman?"

"On TV last night. That is sure one pretty dress you got." Ossie beamed with pleasure.

"On television?" Barbara asked in confusion. Then she remembered the reporters and television cameras outside the benefit. She recovered her composure and laughed. "I'm surprised that your grandmother lets you stay up that late. Don't you go to bed before the eleven o'clock news?''

"Sometimes Grannie falls asleep watching TV," Ossie replied. "Then I can stay up long as I want."

"I see," Barbara said uncomfortably. "I'll tell you something, Ossie. If you want to be a dancer like Mr. Allen, you need your sleep. I think you ought to go to bed a little earlier, even if your grandmother falls asleep. If you burn the candle at both ends, you'll always come up short."

Ossie rolled his eyes at Barbara's typically adult advice, losing interest in the conversation. "Be seeing you, Miz D.," he said as he started to back away. Barbara watched him leave and steeled herself for the inevitable confrontation with Brad.

# Chapter Six

❦

Brad followed Barbara to her office, closing the door behind him. She sat down at her desk and moved some papers around, pretending that Brad wasn't there, but he wouldn't let her forget. "What the hell did you think you were doing last night?"

"I had a date," Barbara replied innocently.

"Not quite," Brad said sarcastically, "I had a date last night—you had a media event."

"Stop it, Brad," Barbara said with an angry flush rising to her cheeks. "Since when is what I do on my own time any concern of yours?"

"It was none of my concern at all until I innocently turned on my television to watch the news and there you were, hanging on the arm of that sleazy politician."

"I'm over twenty-one," Barbara exclaimed, "I can go out with whomever I please."

"Don't you realize what you've done?"

"I went out and had a nice time," Barbara replied calmly, forcing herself to be rational; in a conversation with Brad, someone had to maintain their composure.

"From now on, whenever anyone mentions the Thirty-seventh Street Center, someone else will say, 'Isn't that that place run by Morgan Newman's girl-friend?' " Brad said bitterly.

"That's better than what they were saying before I met Morgan. Then, whenever anyone mentioned the Center someone else would say, 'What's that?' "

"I realize you may be blinded by post-adolescent infatuation, but I would think that even you would real-ize you're being used, Barbara," Brad said, his words laced with sarcasm.

"Morgan has been nothing but good for me and the Center," she said evenly. "If you weren't so blinded by your knee-jerk hostility, you'd realize that."

"Oh yes, he's a real servant of humanity," Brad sneered. "Can't you see that he'll get all the benefits and you'll just get stuck holding the bag? From now on, when we do something good around here, he's going to get all the credit. We'll be known as the Newman Center for the Performing Arts."

"That's ridiculous," Barbara replied with a frown. "We're becoming well known—that's what's important. Do you think you're going to have Calvin Foundation funds forever? The grant we're using here is a one-shot deal. When this money runs out, you're going to have to raise your own funds, Brad. In case you haven't figured it out, you won't be able to raise bus fare if people don't know what the Thirty-seventh Street Center is." Despite her resolve to stay calm, Barbara's voice rose an octave and her cheeks began to burn.

"I don't care!" Brad exclaimed angrily. His voice was rising in volume with each reply he gave. "I will not have my name or the name of my Center mentioned in the same breath with that shifty-eyed crook."

Barbara could maintain her composure no longer.

She stood up and slammed her fist down on the desk. "That's enough, Brad," she practically shouted. "Whom I choose to date is none of your business. And unless you have specific charges that you can support with hard evidence, I don't want to hear anything else about Morgan!" She glared at Brad across the desk, then took a deep breath, forcing herself to calm down again. "I don't want to fight with you, Brad," she said quietly.

Brad was silent for a moment. He started to turn and leave, but stopped himself and turned back to face Barbara. His face had changed—he was no longer angry. Instead he seemed to be pleading with her.

"Barbara, open your eyes. Everything the man does is calculated to make him look good with the media. Do you think it's by chance that he manages to get a spot on the news at least three times a week? There isn't a sincere bone in his body."

"You don't know him, Brad. You're absolutely right when you say that he plays to the media, but just because he knows how to handle the press doesn't mean he is insincere or dishonest. He's done some wonderful things for this city—and that's not my judgment, everybody I talk to says so. You've got to believe that there are people in politics who are dedicated to making the government better and Morgan is one of them."

Brad replied in an equally calm voice. "You have got to be careful," he said quietly. "If you get too involved with him, you could be hurt."

"I appreciate your concern, but I'm a big girl, Brad. I can take care of myself."

"I wish I could believe you," Brad sighed. "I'm sorry if what I've said is out of line, but I care about what happens to you. I don't have a lot of close friends, but you're one of them. You've got class, lady, and you deserve a lot better than what he's going to give you."

"Brad, I care about you, too," Barbara said softly, "but sometimes I wonder how you can be so angry and suspicious all the time. You don't have to fight the world twenty-four hours a day. If you could just put as much effort into being happy as you do into being angry, I think you'd find out that there are as many nice things in the world as there are nasty ones. If you go looking for the good, you'll find it."

"I thought we were talking about you," Brad replied shaking his head.

"I know about fighting," Barbara said. "Do you think I could have gotten any of the respect I get from the Calvin Foundation Board if I didn't know how to fight? Do you think that the stodgy old bankers and lawyers who make up the rest of the board would have given one cent to the Center if I hadn't gotten behind this project and pushed? Brad, there comes a time when you've got to stop fighting and accept what's given to you."

"Nothing is free," he replied. "If there's one thing I've learned in my life, it's that when somebody offers you something for free, it's probably time to start running for the exit. Sooner or later, Morgan Newman is going to come to you looking for payment—and I don't have my mind in the gutter, either. I'm talking about your good name. Are you ready to stand behind whatever he does? Are you ready to have your name and the name of the Calvin Foundation linked with his, no matter what he's involved in? The Calvin Foundation stands for humanitarianism and culture. Are you ready to let him use that name to get elected again?"

"How can I make you understand? I know more about the realities of politics than you seem to think," Barbara said gently. "But my friendship with him has nothing to do with politics. I can't help the fact that what I do privately is going to color how people perceive the Thirty-seventh Street Center and the Calvin Foundation. I won't let institutions, no matter how good, shape my private life. The Center and the foundation are things. I'm a person and people are more important than things. Let's have a truce, Brad. I realize you're thinking about my welfare, but let's put the subject off limits for now."

"All right," Brad said with resignation. "But be careful."

Barbara smiled. "Don't worry about me. I'll be fine."

When Brad turned and left the office, Barbara sat down to get some work done. She tried to narrow her concentration to the papers in front of her, but found that her mind wouldn't cooperate. Staring blankly at the resumé of a music teacher who was applying for a job at the Center, her thoughts kept returning to Brad's accusations—she couldn't dismiss them as easily as she wanted to.

Barbara knew that what she had said to Brad had more to do with arguing than with her feelings. Brad had attacked, and Barbara had defended herself and Morgan. Now, with no one to argue with but herself, she had to look at her feelings in a more impartial light.

The past eight years of Barbara's life had been dedicated to the Calvin Foundation; she had taken her place on the board upon graduating from college. In those years, she had subordinated everything in her life to the goals of the foundation, long ago giving up her personal social life. The young men she dated were a carefully chosen group. She called them friends and cautiously held them at arm's length.

But she had broken every rule she lived by in the case of Morgan Newman. From the moment he kissed her on the sidewalk outside the Center, she had known he wasn't interested in a casual or businesslike friendship, and she had accepted his advances eagerly. Why, after years of subordinating herself to the foundation, had she said to Brad, "I won't let institutions, no matter how good, shape my private life?"

As she puzzled over her own behavior, Barbara realized that she had to come to a decision about what kind of role Morgan was going to play in her life.

However difficult, she had to set aside those confusing physical sensations that robbed her of reason, and make a decision based on what was best for her future—and, as much as she felt like denying it, the futures of the Calvin Foundation and the Thirty-seventh Street Center as well. She couldn't go on pretending that what she did today had nothing to do with tomorrow. Brad's accusations had to be weighed in an objective light. Her own feelings had to be taken into account and weighed against the good of her foundation and the Center.

It was true that Morgan's image was in no way hurt by being seen with her. On the other hand, it wasn't as if she were famous. Few people had any idea who she was or what she did for a living. Therefore, he couldn't be benefiting much from being seen with her, Barbara reasoned. However, he was going out of his way to make her well known, and while the Center was being helped by that exposure, it was almost as if Morgan was trying to make people believe that the Center was one of his own accomplishments.

"So what?" Barbara asked out loud. What did it matter who took the credit as long as something good was accomplished—especially if giving Morgan the credit could help him accomplish more good things in the future?

And what of making it look as if the Calvin Foundation supported Councilman Newman? Had she implied support by going to the benefit dinner with him? Barbara frowned as she contemplated the question. She had never publicly vocalized support of his political stance. In fact, when the television cameras had been on, she hadn't said a single word. How could her actions be interpreted as anything other than personal support?

That left the single most difficult question to be considered. What kind of role was Morgan Newman going to play in her future? Barbara shrank from this last question; there were too many uncertainties in it. Did Morgan feel the same way about her as she did about him? Could she change her lifestyle to focus on another person rather than herself and her work? And, more important, did she want to try?

"I'm getting nowhere," Barbara said to herself as she looked down at the the papers in her hands. She shook the resumé she'd been trying to read and started again at the top, but was mercifully interrupted by the telephone.

"Ms. Danbury, George Leland here," a voice said on the other end of the line.

"Mr. Leland, how nice to hear from you. What can I do for you?" she answered, forcing herself to sound bright and interested.

"Would Monday be a good day for the camera crew to come to the Center and shoot for 'Good Morning Windy City'?" he asked.

Barbara checked the class schedule to make sure there would be enough classes in session that day. "We should have a good variety of classes going then," Barbara replied. "I'll let Mr. Allen know that you're coming."

"Thanks, that will be great. Will you be available on Tuesday morning?" Leland asked.

"It's going to take more than one day?" Barbara asked.

"Not really. What we'd like to do is come out and shoot some tape of the children practicing, then have you come down to the studio for a live interview on Tuesday. We'll show the tape as a part of the interview."

"I think perhaps it's Mr. Allen that you should be interviewing, Mr. Leland," Barbara replied carefully. "I wouldn't want my own part in the Center overemphasized. Mr. Allen conceived the idea and has been the main force in setting it up. My only part in the Center is to protect the interests of the Calvin Foundation."

"Well, ah, yes," Leland said hesitantly, "then maybe both of you should come down for the interview."

"Mr. Allen is very articulate," Barbara insisted. "I think he should be the one to talk about the Center."

There was a moment of silence at the other end of the line while Leland tried to think of a new attack. "I think you could add some extra depth to the piece, Ms. Danbury. You'd be able to tell us something about the foundation behind the Center. Horace Calvin was a fascinating man, and in many ways the Calvin Foundation carries the mark of the man. I don't think we could do a really meaningful piece about the Center without your participation."

Barbara sighed. She knew she was loosing this battle. The segment on "Good Morning Windy City" was too important to the Center for her to drag her heels and possibly lose the opportunity. Yet, she was sure that the reason George Leland wanted to put her in the interview had very little to do with the performing arts. She had an uncomfortable feeling that she was about to be displayed as "Morgan Newman's girlfriend."

"All right, Mr. Leland," Barbara said with resignation. "I'll be happy to cooperate in any way I can."

"Wonderful," Leland replied. "The camera crews will be at the Center by eleven o'clock Monday morning. I look forward to seeing you then."

"Until Monday," Barbara replied before hanging up.

The taping session at the Center went smoothly on Monday. When the television crew arrived the Advanced Modern Dance class was in session and performed beautifully. Brad was beaming with pride as the best students the Center had went through their paces for the cameras.

But, as well as the taped portion of the students went, Barbara looked toward the live interview with growing dread. John LeClair, the program's host, had a reputation for constantly putting guests on the spot with his questions, and Barbara was nervous about what he was going to ask her. She had made it a point to watch the program several times since Mr. Leland's call, only to see LeClair flustering his guests with sudden, seemingly unrelated questions. Again and again the guests were thrown off balance and they revealed things they hadn't intended to.

Barbara had an extra weight on her mind Tuesday morning when she reported to the television studio with Brad. The public's perception of her as Morgan Newman's girlfriend had been reenforced when her Saturday night date with Morgan had turned into an impromptu press conference outside the restaurant where they'd had dinner. Morgan had apologized to her afterward, saying that he had never intended their date to become so public. But Barbara found herself harboring a nagging suspicion that he had actually planned to meet the reporters; his answers to their questions had seemed much too precise to be truly off the cuff.

The incident added to her confusion about her future with Morgan. At first, Barbara had resented the idea of the press following her every move in public. But when she and Morgan had returned to his apartment, her resentment had been swept away by the fulfillment they had found in the beauty and intimacy of each other. And afterward, she felt like she was in a house of mirrors. Barbara couldn't be sure which was the real Morgan Newman—the public man whose every move was directed for the benefit of the press, or the private man who touched her and made the earth move.

After they had made love, when Barbara rested against the warm pillow of his chest, Morgan asked her if she was happy. In that moment, she could only answer that she was, but something in her voice made him take notice and ask her what was wrong.

"I don't know," she said uncertainly. "Was that business with the reporters tonight really necessary?"

Morgan sighed. "I can't fool you for a minute, can I? Yes, I think it was necessary. I have to take every chance I can get with the press right now."

"I wish we could have some time just to ourselves," Barbara replied softly. "Without having reporters following us around."

"The election is coming up in November," Morgan explained patiently. "Right now, I have to keep myself in front of the public, so they won't forget me in November."

Barbara laughed in spite of herself. "How could anybody forget the great Morgan Newman?" She regretted the sarcastic ring to her voice, but there was a feeling of hurt deep within her.

"Barbara, you mean a great deal to me—even though

we've only known each other a short time. I wouldn't hurt you for the world. Please be patient. The November election is special, probably the most important election I've ever been in. I can't tell you why, yet, but it's going to change everything—for both of us. Just bear with me through this and I promise you, you won't be sorry."

Then, when he kissed her again, the hurt was gone and she only wanted her time with him to go on forever.

Now, in the harsh incandescent light of the television studio, she wished she had chosen a different course. John LeClair would be zeroing in on her. She would have a double problem during the interview; not only must she protect the Center from any adverse publicity stemming from her personal life, she also had to protect Morgan's reputation. LeClair would be trying to trip her up—to get her to say something embarrassing or revealing about Morgan. George Leland might be Morgan's friend, but Barbara knew enough about television journalism to know that, as soon as the cameras were turned on, she was fair game for whatever LeClair could get her to say.

Brad, on the other hand, was the picture of composure. He was wearing a dark gray suit with a blue-and-gray striped tie. Barbara had never seen him in a suit before and was impressed with his dapper appearance. He walked onto the talk show set with the confidence of the seasoned performer he was.

"You're as pale as a ghost," Brad whispered to her as they waited to go on. "Are you all right?"

"I'm fine," Barbara said as firmly as she could. "Just a little jittery. You, on the other hand, look fantastic. Where have you been hiding that suit?"

Brad's face broke into a toothy grin. "You like the threads, eh? Just got them."

Barbara fidgeted with the clasp on her purse for a moment, then started looking around for a water fountain. Her mouth felt as if it were lined with cotton.

"Don't let this guy spook you," Brad said softly. "Just forget about the camera and relax. If you don't get nervous, he can't make you say anything you don't want to."

"You sound like a veteran of this sort of thing—oh, I forgot, you are, aren't you? I remember seeing you once on 'The Phil Donahue Show' back when you were with the Mid-States Ballet Company."

"That's right. Just remember, compared to Donahue, this guy is bush league."

Barbara smiled and took a deep breath. The director signaled for a commercial break and John LeClair looked straight into the camera. "We'll be back after these messages with Brad Allen and Barbara Danbury to talk about a unique project for the youth of the Thirty-seventh Street area." The director cued a technician at the electronic console and part of the tape taken the day before at the Center appeared on the monitor before the show faded out to the commercial.

"You're on next," the director said to Barbara and Brad, ushering them into a set of comfortable chairs next to John LeClair's desk. The set was uncomfortably hot under the glare of the studio lights and Barbara felt a drop of perspiration form and run down her back under her cream-colored silk blouse. LeClair, a solidly built middle-aged man with short, steel gray hair and deep blue eyes, was busying himself with a quick review of his notes. "Fifteen seconds, John," the director said, and LeClair's head came up to greet the camera.

"I have with me two people who are determined to do the impossible," LeClair said smoothly. "Not many people would go looking for the next Baryshnikov in a decaying Chicago neighborhood, but that is exactly

what Brad Allen and Barbara Danbury are doing." The
camera angle widened out to include Barbara and Brad
in the shot. "The Thirty-seventh Street Center for the
performing Arts is unusual in several respects," LeClair
continued. "Perhaps the most unusual is that it is
costing the taxpayers of Chicago absolutely nothing.
This entirely privately-funded school is offering opportunities to Chicago youngsters that were never available
before. Mr. Allen, just one year ago, you were being considered for the position of creative director for the Mid-
States Ballet. Why did you give up that opportunity in
favor of a dance school for disadvantaged children?"

Brad smiled easily. "First, let me say that the Thirty-
seventh Street Center is more than just a dance school.
We offer lessons in music, voice, and drama as well as
dance. But to answer your question, I think you've
answered it better than I ever could. When I was a child,
the opportunities for a poor child to study ballet were
very limited. Think of how many important talents
have been wasted because training and encouragement
weren't available. When the time came for me to retire
from the stage, I had to ask myself where I could do the
most good, choreographing for a company that can
afford to hire the best talent available, or back with my
roots, offering opportunities to the next generation of
performers."

Barbara sat completely still, letting Brad have all the
attention. The words flowed from him in a confident,
relaxed stream, and for several minutes, LeClair was
content to talk exclusively to Brad. Barbara hoped that
this would continue throughout the interview, and her
hopes were bolstered when the segment was half over
and the videotape shot at the Center had been shown.
So far Barbara had managed to remain almost invisible
in front of the camera. In an odd way she was amused

with herself. Being invisible on camera was getting to be a habit with her. That's how it always was when Morgan was giving his interviews. However, after the next commercial break, LeClair turned to her abruptly.

"Ms. Danbury, this project represents a major departure for the Calvin Foundation, doesn't it?"

Barbara took a deep breath and found the confident voice she always used in the boardroom. "Yes, but I hope we can look upon this as the direction we will be taking more often in the future. The Thirty-seventh Street Center is proving itself to be even more worthwhile than we had hoped."

"When the original grant runs out, will the Center be looking for city funds to continue?" LeClair asked blandly. Barbara's heart jumped. This was it, the opener question that could lead to questions about her relationship with Morgan. Before she could answer, Brad came to her rescue.

"We don't anticipate any city participation in our Center," Brad said smoothly. "The idea behind the Center is to offer the quality of private-school lessons to children who otherwise couldn't afford them. We have no intention of becoming one more division of the City Recreation Department. As long as our funding is private, we can maintain private quality."

LeClair recovered gracefully from having his attack blocked. "Ms. Danbury, I understand you were present at the recent Clean Up Our Parks benefit. Do you see any kind of alliance between the Parks Committee and your Center?"

Barbara was ready for this attack. "We've been talking with Tom Staley about a series of recitals in the parks," she said evenly. "However, that may not get started until next summer."

"Councilman Newman has been a very active participant in the Parks Committee," LeClair replied. "Has he had any part in arranging your agreement?"

Barbara kept her face carefully composed. This would be a critical answer. She glanced at Brad out of the corner of her eye, but found no help. "Councilman Newman has been very interested in our work at the Center," she said carefully. "But because of his commitments, he has very little time to spare for us. However, all that he has contributed has been deeply appreciated."

"And just what has the councilman contributed?" LeClair pressed.

"His encouragement," Barbara replied.

LeClair seemed to be winding up for another attack when the director held up his hand to signal another commercial. LeClair made a smooth transition to announcing the next segment and Barbara let out her breath in relief. When the camera was turned off, LeClair thanked them and turned back to his notes. Barbara and Brad got up to leave.

"I knew you could do it," Brad said under his breath. "You handled him like a trouper."

"Ha! You handled him. You took twice as much time as you needed to answer every question he asked you, so when he came to me, he ran out of time," Barbara replied. "Thank you."

"Anything for the cause," Brad said with a wide smile.

# Chapter Seven

The doorman at Morgan's apartment building smiled when he saw Barbara coming. She and Bogey had become a regular visitors, and the doorman liked dogs, especially those that weighed less than ten pounds. Bogey strained at the end of his leash as he saw his large, uniformed friend standing at the curb. He knew that the deep pockets of the doorman's quasi-military coat usually contained a treat.

"And how are you today, Ms. Danbury?" the doorman asked casually, pretending to ignore Bogey, who was dancing on his hind legs.

Barbara shifted the sack of groceries she was carrying, to get a better grip on it, and smiled. "Just fine, and you?" She replied politely. Bogey decided that he could wait no longer for his treat and let out a sharp yap as he pawed the doorman's leg.

"Excellent, Ms. Danbury, excellent," the doorman replied. "But what's this? Are you attempting to bring a mouse on a leash into my building?" With his hands on his hips and his eyes open wide in mock surprise, he looked down at Bogey.

"Is that against the rules?" Barbara asked, going along with the game. "All it says on the sign in the lobby is that all pets must be on leashes."

"I think we can allow it in your case," the doorman replied gravely. "Of course, if you would feed this animal properly, he might grow up to be a Great Dane." He rummaged through his pockets and found the liver-flavored treat, bending over to offer it to Bogey.

Barbara laughed. "He's going to become as fat as a piglet just off the goodies you keep giving him."

The doorman held the door for Barbara as she went into the lobby, then went ahead of her to press the elevator button for her. "Have a nice evening, Ms. Danbury," he said with a smile and an approving nod as the elevator doors closed. Barbara balanced her sack of groceries on the handrail in the elevator and pressed the button for Morgan's floor.

Barbara couldn't help but be amused by the friendly doorman. He made no secret of his belief that Morgan was ever so much wiser now that he was dating her exclusively, than he had been when he was dating every woman in town. If only Brad were so approving, she mused. Since the television show, Brad had refrained from making any comment about her relationship with Morgan, but that didn't mean he was offering silent approval. Barbara could tell by his scowl on the mornings after she had been seen with Morgan on television that Brad's disapproval was as strong as ever.

And she had been seen with Morgan quite frequently. Seldom did they go anywhere in public where they weren't followed by the press. Barbara was getting used to it, in a way. She still felt uncomfortable in the center of a crowd of clamoring reporters, but she had developed a habit of simply tuning out as soon as the press came on the scene. She would stand next to Morgan and smile blandly as he made whatever statement he had prepared—all the time letting her mind wander to other places and subjects, usually the anticipation of the time when she and Morgan would be alone.

She never spoke to the reporters who surrounded Morgan. Yet, her position as Morgan's exclusive companion had brought her a certain notoriety. She was treading a thin line between anonymity and celebrity these days. She did all she could to use her new-found fame to the advantage of the Center, but when gossip columnists called her and asked for an "exclusive" about Morgan, she always politely refused to comment. One columnist, known only as The Keyhole, had dubbed her Barbara No-Comment-But-If-You'd-Like-To-Talk-About-My-Work Danbury. Soon after, when The Keyhole had confidently reported that Barbara would be wearing an engagement ring soon and the wedding would take place right after the election, a reporter asked Morgan during one of his press conferences to comment on his marriage plans. Morgan had smiled and commented that he put very little faith in news coming from anyone who wouldn't even reveal his true name. The reporter had persisted, turning to Barbara and asking if she would be marrying soon. Barbara smiled and said, "No comment, but if you'd like to talk about my work . . ." The reporters laughed and with the next question returned to Morgan's work in The city council.

As the elevator rose through the apartment building, Barbara reflected on how well the summer was going. The Center was approaching the point where it was almost taking on a life of its own. More people were getting involved, taking some of the burden of work off

herself and Brad and leaving her with ample time to
spend with Morgan. In the first week of July, when the
temperatures had stayed in the nineties for six days
straight, Brad had scrounged up an old, dilapidated air
conditioner and suddenly the Center had become the
place to be for every neighborhood child who couldn't
get to the municipal swimming pool. The sudden influx
of children taxed their facilities, but Brad maintained
that it was worth the trouble to deal with a hundred
drop-in students, if he could find one child with an
undeveloped talent.

As the Center became better known partially through
Barbara's new-found fame and partially through her
efforts at getting publicity, new sponsors were turning
up. A construction company whose president was a
patron of the arts had donated soundproofing for the
music practice rooms. A major corporation committed
itself to paying the salary of a drama teacher on a
continuing basis, and, just this week an anonymous
donor had paid to install floor-to-ceiling mirrors along
one wall of the dance studio. The Center was coming
close to the point where it would be self-supporting, no
longer needing the Calvin Foundation's help. Barbara
knew that the time when her job would be finished here
was fast approaching, but she preferred not to think
about that eventuality.

She wanted these summer days to stretch on forever,
because for once in her life she was completely happy,
as if she had discovered something completely original.
She wondered how she could have lived so long without experiencing the fulfillment she felt when she was
with Morgan. Barbara had stopped torturing herself
with questions about whether Morgan was sincere and
whether she was doing the right thing by being seen
with him. She only had to look into his eyes when they

were alone to know that he *was* sincere, and the publicity rolled off her back like water off a duck.

When the elevator doors opened on the top floor, Barbara stepped out and led Bogey down the hall to Morgan's door. She rang the buzzer with her elbow, and Morgan appeared momentarily to relieve her of her bundles.

"What have we here?" he asked, peeking into the sack before he took it into the kitchen and started unloading it.

Barbara named the items as he set them out. "Trout, almonds, white wine—domestic, but respectable label—fresh green beans, and eggs. For the souffle," she announced.

"*Madame*, you spoil me," Morgan said teasingly.

"I'm not so dumb," Barbara replied. "I've figured out that the only way I can have you completely to myself for an entire meal is to cook for you here."

"Ah, but is the lady safe, alone with me in my lair?" Morgan asked, standing behind Barbara and putting his arms around her waist. He nuzzled the base of her neck and took the lobe of her ear gently between his teeth, making Barbara's pulse beat faster.

"I'm as safe as I could please," Barbara said with a light chuckle. "I brought my chaperone with me. If you get out of line, Bogey will come after you."

"Your chaperone is awfully easy to bribe," Morgan teased. "All I have to do is put a bowl of table scraps out on the patio and we won't see him again until morning."

"That's what's so good about him as a chaperone," Barbara replied. "He knows when to get lost. But seriously, if you don't let go of me the fish will spoil before I get it cooked."

"Pity. Next time bring something that won't spoil so

quickly, like beef jerky," Morgan replied as he reluc-
tantly let her go.

"Yuck," Barbara said as she began to prepare dinner.
"If you want beef jerky find yourself an Eskimo
woman."

Later, as Barbara brought the trout almondine to the
table on the patio, and Morgan pulled the cork from the
bottle of wine, Barbara had a sudden feeling of right-
ness. These simple tasks of cooking and setting a table,
joining her man in a delicious meal, then doing the
dishes afterward—Morgan drying and putting them
away as she washed—carried an inexplicable satisfaction. She wished that she could cook for Morgan every
night, not just once or twice a week. She deliberately
refused to think about the time when her work in
Chicago would be done and she would return to New
York.

That evening, they sat on the patio long after dinner
was over and watched the sun sink behind the cityscape. As the sky darkened from shades of orange to
crimson to violet, and the lights came on, Morgan
talked about a committee meeting he had gone to that
day and Barbara listened lazily, without really paying
much attention, simply letting the sound of his voice
surround her like music.

"And I'm going to back legislation that requires every
woman in the city to dye her hair red and wear false
eyelashes," Morgan said in an even voice.

"That sounds like a good idea," Barbara replied dis-
tantly.

Morgan got up and came around the table to face Barbara and looked directly into her eyes. "You haven't
heard a word I've said!" he exclaimed.

Barbara snapped out of her half-conscious state and
smiled guiltily. "Sorry, I guess I was daydreaming."

"You sure know how to make a guy feel boring."

"I feel too good tonight to talk about committee meetings," Barbara replied.

"Then what shall we talk about? Name a subject."

"Cabbages and kings, and why the sea is boiling hot and whether pigs have wings," Barbara said dreamily.

"I don't think you want to talk at all," Morgan said softly, a husky quality entering his voice. He reached down and took her hand to pull her up into his arms. He kissed her warmly and stroked her red curls. "If I let you go on, you'll probably start reciting 'How Doth the Little Crocodile.' "

"No, but if I let you go on, you'll be reciting the city budget," Barbara said, returning his kisses and wrapping her arms around his neck.

"In that case, I'm going to pass a law against talking for the rest of the night," Morgan said as he led her from the patio to his bedroom. Bogey curled up in his favorite spot next to the base of the potted dwarf cherry tree on the patio and buried his nose in his tail, content to wait for morning.

On a morning not long after, Barbara walked into the Center and was surprised to find it empty of children. The spacious dance studio was deserted except for the brooding figure of Brad, who was sitting on a three-legged stool near the mirror wall. Dressed in his usual ragged T-shirt and sweatpants, arms crossed against his chest, he had a look on his face that made the hair on Barbara's neck stand on end. She glanced furtively at her watch and confirmed the fact that it was ten o'clock, there should be a dance class going on, and other students should be practicing their music. But the room was silent and Brad seemed to project his anger throughout it. He glowered at Barbara but didn't say a word.

Steeling herself for whatever was coming she crossed the room. "Where are the students?"

"I sent them home," Brad replied with narrowed eyes and flaring nostrils. Barbara felt her stomach twist. As much as she admired and cared for Brad, she dreaded his unpleasant side.

"Is there some problem?" Barbara asked quietly.

"*Is there some problem?*" Brad shouted in reply. Then he stopped and lowered his voice, speaking with deadly precision through his clenched jaw. "I don't believe it. You know, Barbara, I tried to convince myself that you were just blinded by Newman's charm, that sooner or later you were going to wake up and see what was really going on. But I never thought I'd see you sell out everything we've worked so hard for."

"What on earth are you talking about?" Barbara asked plaintively.

"Stop playing dumb," Brad snarled. "You may be two-faced, but I know for a fact that you're not stupid."

"Even a criminal has a right to know what he's being accused of," Barbara said with a tremor in her voice.

"I'm talking about the Inner City Industrial Park!" Brad snapped.

"The what?"

"Stop it. How can you pretend you don't know what I'm talking about? You were standing right there."

"Where? And what does an industrial park have to do with sending the children home?"

Brad's features took on a look of amazement. It was slowly dawning on him that Barbara wasn't faking anything; she really didn't know what he was talking about. He got off his stool silently and went to the middle of the studio where a newspaper lay crumpled on the floor. He picked it up and smoothed out a few of the wrinkles before he shoved it into Barbara's hands. It was the morning edition and Barbara gasped as she read the banner headline,

"COUNCIL GIVES GO-AHEAD
TO 38TH STREET INDUSTRIAL DISTRICT."

Neatly tucked under the headline was a large photograph of Morgan Newman with Barbara at his side. A numb feeling started to spread through her as she read the article. She remembered the picture being taken last night as they left the symphony concert and Morgan gave his usual press conference on the steps of the hall. But she hadn't the slightest idea what he had talked about. As was her habit, she had simply tuned out for as long as the reporters were surrounding them. She glanced at the picture again and winced at the insipid smile on her own face.

The Chicago City Council voted yesterday to rezone the area from 38th Street to 42nd Street and from Wyler Boulevard to Brown Street, for industrial use only. The move follows Amalgamated Manufacturing's request for a site within the city limits on which to build a new factory, which the company claims will be the largest of its kind ever built within a metropolitan area and will employ more than 4,000 skilled and unskilled workers.

After two weeks of debate, the council approved the Newman plan, which calls for the clearing of sixteen blocks of substandard housing to make way for the new industrial park.

"The area in question has long been a pocket of low employment and high welfare," Councilman Morgan Newman said of his plan yesterday evening. "We're going to reverse that. The Inner City Industrial Park is going to become a model for the revitalization of our cities. It's time we started looking for ways to lure industries back to where the people are, for the good of the city and the people."

The article continued, reporting a schedule for the demolition of the neighborhood, but Barbara didn't bother to read the rest. The words, "for the good of the city and the people," stuck in her head. When she read them, she could hear Morgan's rich, authoritative voice. Her own voice was paralyzed now as the newspaper fell from her hands and Barbara turned from Brad's accusing stare.

He walked to the front door and gestured toward the doomed neighboorhood. "Why don't you come take a last look at the homes of most of our students?" he asked bitterly. "By next summer they'll be scattered in low-cost housing projects throughout the city. Your Mr. Newman looks out this direction and all he sees is 'substandard housing.' Do you want to know what I see? I see a neighborhood where people know each other, where children have been growing up for generations, where people still have some hope of bettering themselves. Do you have any concept of what those low-cost housing projects are like? And what are we supposed to do here at the Center? Should I start planning dance workshops for factory workers on their lunch hours?"

"I don't know, Brad," Barbara said weakly.

"Barbara, stop standing there looking like an abandoned child," Brad said in a gentler tone of voice. "How could you know nothing of this?"

"I guess I wasn't paying any attention," Barbara sighed. She glanced down at the newspaper at her feet and her own face looked back at her. The horrible, dumb smile hit her like a slap in the face and she impulsively kicked the newspaper away.

"Taking it out on the newspaper won't change the facts," Brad said with a note of dejection in his voice. "I already tried that."

In the wake of the humiliation of finding out what she had been silently supporting, a tide of anger rose in Barbara. She stomped off to her office and slammed the door behind her. After sweeping every piece of paper on her desk onto the floor, she kicked the filing cabinet violently. The pain that the kick brought to her foot helped her to focus on her thoughts and get control of herself. She turned around and found that Brad had followed her into the office and was looking at her in amazement.

"Are you all right?" he asked.

"Better than you know," Barbara said coldly. "Call me a taxi. I'm going down to city hall."

She rode downtown in a state of cold fury, and swept through the lobby of city hall without looking to either side. More than one person had to jump out of her way as she made a straight shot for the elevator.

Sylvia looked up in surprise as Barbara strode into Morgan's suite. "Mr. Newman is in conference," the secretary said ineffectually as Barbara went straight for Morgan's office door. "You'll have to wait. Hey!" Barbara ignored her, yanked open the door and went inside.

Ron Caldwell was standing next to Morgan's desk pointing out something on a map spread in front of the seated councilman. The two men looked at Barbara in surprise as she stormed into the office. After a moment of shock, Morgan smiled his most charming smile.

"Barbara, what a nice surprise. If you could just wait outside a minute . . ."

Barbara turned to Ron Caldwell and spoke in a voice

of pure ice. "Come back later. Mr. Newman will be tied up for a while."

Caldwell started at her peremptory order. At first he frowned and looked as if he was going to stand his ground, but Barbara gave him such a withering look that he changed his mind and, grabbing the map from Morgan's desk, almost ran from the room.

"What's the meaning of this?" Morgan asked with a touch of impatience in his voice. "I do have work to do."

"What is the meaning of this?" Barbara snapped. "Why don't *you* tell *me*?"

Morgan sighed and took on the look of an adult dealing with an intractable child. "We'll get this over with much more quickly if you tell me what's upsetting you," he said in an infuriatingly condescending tone.

"How *could* you?" Barbara fumed. "All the time you were showing me off all over town, you were secretly plotting behind my back to destroy everything Brad and I have accomplished here."

"Barbara, what on earth are you talking about?" Morgan replied in frustration.

"I'm talking about the Amalgamated Manufacturing plant!" she exclaimed.

"That has nothing to do with you," Morgan said with a frown.

"Oh, doesn't it? Just what do you think we're going to do for students after you tear down their homes and scatter them all over the city in low-cost housing projects?"

For a moment Morgan just looked dumbly at Barbara, then his brow knit and his frown deepened. "Oh, I love this," he said in a voice that gathered gravity as he continued. "You burst into my office in the middle of an important conference to fly in my face about an issue that has finally been settled after *weeks* of debate. How did I secretly plot against you? Every word of the controversy about where that factory was going to be located has been reported in the newspapers and on television. I made several statements on the subject while you were standing right beside me. I guess it was just too boring for you to listen to what I was saying."

Barbara knew she was guilty of not paying attention when Morgan was talking politics, but at the moment, she was too angry to accept any culpability. She glared back at him. "You're going to destroy the Center," she said angrily. "More than half our students live in the area you're going to clear."

"Where were you when the subject was open for debate?" Morgan retorted. "We held public hearings right there in the neighborhood to give the residents an opportunity for input. Where were you when I was pounding the pavement looking for a reason not to clear that area?"

"I never heard anything about a public hearing," Barbara said uncertainly.

"We published notices for the hearings in the newspapers three separate times—just like the law says. But of course, nobody reads the public announcements in the newspapers—they're so boring. Do you realize that the night we met, I had just finished waiting for two hours in an empty meeting hall, hoping that someone would show up for a public hearing? Where were you then?"

"You can't just knock down homes and send the people away," Barbara replied. "And how can you destroy everything I've been working for?"

"Oh, excuse me—I'm sorry I failed to recognize the importance of the work you're doing. After all, teaching pre-adolescent punks to dance is so significant, especially when you compare it to something as trivial as putting thousands of unemployed men back to work so they can feed their families," Morgan said sarcastically.

If Barbara's temper had been settling down, this last remark only renewed her fury. "That factory would employ just as many people if it were located outside the city where you wouldn't have to tear down any homes to build it! But then you wouldn't be able to take credit for saving all those poor families from starvation, would you?"

"If you're accusing me of putting the good of the city ahead of everything else, you're absolutely correct. If I can get an industry to locate inside the city, I'm adding to our tax revenues. I'm putting people back to work, and I'm ridding the city of a blighted neighborhood," Morgan replied confidently.

"A blighted neighborhood. Is that all you see? That neighborhood can be saved, Morgan. That's why we located there. It still has a strong base of families. If you weren't so terrified of being robbed that you lock your wallet in the car whenever you go there, you might be able to see that if those people could only find some pride in themselves and their neighborhood, they could pull together and repair the decay. That's what the Thirty-seventh Street Center is all about."

"And I suppose they can all pirouette and do ballet leaps as they're running around fixing up their apartments?" Morgan sneered. "You are so naive. I suppose you've never been robbed in that neighborhood? Did you just give your bag to that purse snatcher to be friendly?"

Barbara felt a sinking feeling in her stomach. She didn't want to argue anymore, she just wanted to get away—away from Morgan's sickening cynicism and away from her own heartbreaking disillusionment. She had to force herself to keep her voice steady as unwanted tears filled her eyes. "Why that particular neighborhood? There are worse areas."

"Because it's close to several large access streets that can carry the extra burden of traffic and the sewer system in that area can handle an industrial load without any upgrading. Plus, the area is a health and safety nightmare. Surely you've noticed that there are more rats in the neighborhood than people? It's just a matter of time before someone whose electricity has been turned off knocks over a candle and starts a fire that will kill hundreds. There isn't a thing worth saving in that whole sixteen-block area." Morgan had taken hold of himself and was now speaking in a more reasonable tone.

"You forget," Barbara said coldly. "I live on Forty-First Street."

"Barbara," he pleaded. "You've got to understand. No matter what our relationship is, I've got to do what's best for the city. Let's not fight this way . . ."

Barbara stepped back from the front of his desk. She was revolted by the smooth way Morgan dismissed her objections and expected her to forget what he was doing and come back to him. She couldn't bear to be in the same room with his cynicism, and though she wanted to say a thousand angry things to him, her voice seemed to be paralyzed. Finally, all she could force herself to say was, "I hope you and your city are very happy together." Then she turned on her heel and left his office, sweeping past Sylvia without even looking at the perplexed woman.

Barbara went directly home in a taxi, trembling all the way and willing herself not to cry. The driver kept glancing in his rearview mirror to look at her with a worried expression, and when she got out to pay him with shaking hands, he asked her if she was all right or if she would like him to take her to a doctor. The unexpected kindness in his voice seemed to hurt as badly as Morgan's words had and finally she just handed him a twenty-dollar bill and ran into the apartment building with tears streaming down her cheeks. She ran up the stairs, praying that she wouldn't meet anyone she knew, and at last closed and locked her door behind her.

But even alone in her apartment, Barbara couldn't get away from the terrible hurt. She went into the bedroom, threw herself on her bed, and cried until merciful sleep came to relieve her wounded pride.

It was sometime in the late afternoon when she woke to find Bogey's cold nose probing her ear. She sat up slowly and sighed. "It's time for your walk, isn't it?" she said to her little dog. Her voice felt scratchy and as she looked down at herself she saw that her clothes were rumpled. She picked the little dog up and cradled him in her arms, running her fingers through his silky hair. Bogey turned up his face and licked her cheek appreciatively. "Well, we'll just have to get your leash and take you out," she murmured.

Barbara got the leash from its hook on the kitchen wall and was on her way out when the doorbell rang. Without a thought for who it might be, she drew the deadbolt and opened the door to the last person on earth she wanted to see.

# Chapter Eight

Barbara hesitated for a moment before Morgan's presence completely registered, then she started to slam the door in his face. But her moment of hesitation was enough; rather than the satisfying slam she had hoped for, she only heard a muffled yelp as the door crushed the foot he had put forward.

Morgan immediately pushed the door back open and stepped inside. "Was that enough physical revenge to satisfy your honor?" he moaned as he limped over to her sofa and sat down.

"Go away," Barbara said. "I don't want to see you or talk to you right now."

"Too bad," Morgan said calmly, "because you're going to see me and listen to me whether you want to or not. I have to talk to you, and I'm going to."

"I can always call the police and have you arrested—this time for real," she replied tersely.

"I suppose you could. If you did, it would make a great deal of trouble for me politically. After all, nobody would vote for a man who forces his way into the homes of unwilling women. However, if that's what you're going to do, go ahead. I have no intention of leaving here until I've had my say, no matter what you do."

Barbara hesitated for a moment, unsure of what to do. As angry as she was, she didn't really want to cause him any harm. Finally, she came over and sat down stiffly in the chair opposite the sofa. "Say your piece and get out," she said coldly.

"Barbara, if you don't like what I do as a councilman, don't vote for me. Oh, I know, you're not registered in this city. Well, you could start a petition drive for my recall, or tell the press nasty things about me and make sure I don't get reelected. But whatever you think about my performance as a councilman, don't shut me out of your life. Please."

Barbara was at a loss for a reply. For any argument he could have given her in favor of tearing down the neighborhood, she had two in favor of saving it, but to his simple plea, she had no defense.

Morgan waited for her answer, and when none came, he let out a deep sigh. "I've voted on more than a hundred ordinances since January," he continued. "I have no idea how many times you would have voted with me or how many times against, but I really don't care. For me, this industrial development is no different than the sewer expansion project or the police budget. How I vote in the council has nothing to do with who my friends are." As he spoke, his eyes never left Barbara's face. "All I know is that I've made you cry and I never ever intended to hurt you."

Barbara's hand rose involuntarily to her cheek as she realized that her mascara must be streaked from her earlier tears. She hadn't looked in a mirror since waking. Under the constant pressure of his eyes she finally found her voice. "I understand that you have to vote your conscience," she said in a low voice. "But I never realized that you held my work in such contempt."

"I have never held your work, or anything you've done, in contempt," Morgan replied sincerely. "Actually, I think we've both been guilty of the same sin. We don't pay much attention to one another's work. I've always been aware of your work, but when I'm in the council, I simply never think about the Center. You know that I'm a councilman, but you pay little attention to what I do politically. Our relationship has never had anything to do with the Thirty-seventh Street Center or the Chicago City Council. I can't honestly say whether I'd have done anything different if I *had* considered the effect that the industrial park was going to have on the Center. But the fact is that I never did consider it."

"This morning, everything you said was so . . . cynical," Barbara stammered, finding that tears were rising in her eyes once again.

"I think we both said things this morning that we regret . . ." he responded slowly, searching Barbara's face for some sign of agreement.

"I don't know what to think anymore," Barbara said plaintively. "Suddenly I'm not sure that I really know you at all, Morgan."

"I don't care what you think about my work, but I care a lot about what you think of me as a person. Not the person who gives press conferences and interviews, but the person I am when we're alone together. We've shared something very special, Barbara. Tell me you hate me because I'm a shallow hypocrite, but don't shut me out over a political issue."

"I don't know what to think anymore," Barbara

repeated quietly. "Maybe I just need some time to get a better perspective on the situation."

Morgan rose and came over to where Barbara was sitting. He reached down and took her hands in his own, and their warmth made her realize that her hands were ice cold and trembling. "All right," he said gently. "Take some time and think about it. I won't call you or try to see you until Friday night, on one condition."

Barbara looked up and met his eyes for the first time since he had come into her apartment. "What condition?" she asked dully.

"That on Friday you'll come away with me for the next week."

"I have to work next week," Barbara replied without conviction.

"You can take some time off," Morgan said confidently. "I have a cottage up on Lake Michigan a couple of hours north of here. We can go up for the week and speak of absolutely nothing that exists in the city of Chicago for the entire week. We can spend some time alone together with no telephone, no reporters, no television and no Thirty-seventh Street Center. It will be just you and me. We've never really had much time alone together. Spend some time with just me—then, if you still can't stand me, at least we'll know we tried."

Barbara was mute with indecision. His words seemed to make sense, and the very sound of his voice was comforting, but somehow she couldn't bring herself to give in so easily. Morgan gently pulled her to her feet so that they faced one another equally. "Say yes," he implored.

"I don't know," Barbara replied, casting her eyes at the floor.

"I'll pick you up at seven o'clock Friday," Morgan replied with the purpose that she lacked. "Pack your bathing suit." With that he turned and went to the door.

"And don't forget to wash your face before you take that dog of yours for a walk," he added before he left, closing the door softly behind him.

Morgan was true to his word and made no attempt to contact Barbara before Friday. She spent the remainder of the week in a blue funk, accomplishing very little and finding it difficult to eat or even sleep because of the numbing indecision that had settled over her. Her work at the Center came to a near halt because of the doubts about its future, but Brad continued to conduct classes, reasoning that every lesson the children got in before the Center's demise was one more step in the right direction. Barbara found that she could do little or nothing. There was no point in laying plans for the coming year if the Center might not even exist then. There was no reason to review the resumés of potential teachers when she doubted that anyone would ever be hired.

So Barbara spent as little time at the Center as she could. She sat down and talked to Brad a few times, but found that his lethargic acceptance of the end of his dream only left her feeling worse than before. Once his anger had been spent, Brad changed. Barbara had never imagined that this feisty, determined man could be beaten, but Brad was showing all the signs of giving in. He became lax with the students and between classes he slumped into the chair behind his desk. Barbara felt miserable for him because she knew that the Center had been more his dream than her own. She wished that she could say something to comfort him, but her own feelings were much too battered to leave room for comforting anyone else. She let Brad know that she would be gone during next week, but pointedly omitted the fact that she would be spending the week with Morgan. For all Brad knew, Barbara was about to take a short vacation to revitalize her spirits.

Her feelings about Morgan continued to be confusing. She wasn't even sure why she had agreed to go away with him. When she searched her heart, Barbara found a void where he was concerned. She could remember the ecstasy of his touch and the wonderful satisfaction of lying beside him after they had made love, but the memories were now tainted with the bitter disappointment she had so recently experienced and she couldn't explain the disappointment rationally. It wasn't as if Barbara had discovered anything about Morgan that hadn't been clear from the beginning; she had known from their first afternoon together that Morgan was completely dedicated to his career and that everything else was secondary. She'd also recognized the smooth way he dealt with the press and the public, and had accepted the fact that there were two Morgans, the private and the public. Understanding all that, why was she feeling so lost and betrayed now? Was it possible that she had been deceiving herself all along? Even as she pretended to recognize the truth about Morgan, had she been imagining a perfect version of the man, one that no mortal could live up to?

On Friday afternoon, while she was cleaning off her desk, Brad came into her office wearing his now-customary look of gloom.

"Can I do something for you?" Barbara asked, attempting to sound cheerful but failing miserably.

"No, just have a nice relaxing vacation and don't even think about this mess," he replied without conviction. Barbara felt an extra twinge of guilt, knowing she was going away with the person responsible for making her friend this miserable.

"Maybe it's not as bad as we think," Barbara offered.

"I wish I could think of how," Brad said glumly.

"When I get back, we'll put our heads together and start thinking constructively. We've already spent too much time mourning our own demise. There must be a way around it. Maybe we could hit our sponsors for a couple of buses—then we could pick up our students and take them home after classes . . ." Barbara's voice trailed off as she realized that the plan was totally impractical.

Brad responded with a faint smile that acknowledged her attempt to brighten the atmosphere, but it faded away almost immediately. He didn't even bother to point out the flaws in her plan because he knew that Barbara didn't believe it would work any more than he did.

"It was just a thought," Barbara said, looking back down at her desk to avoid Brad's eyes. "If not that, something else. We can't just lie down and die."

"You go away and get rid of all those cobwebs upstairs," Brad said kindly. "We'll still be here when you come back—for a little while at least."

"Brad, even if this doesn't work out, at least we tried. That's worth something."

Brad regarded Barbara with a sad smile. "This really cost you a lot, didn't it?" he asked quietly.

"It's not my money. I just give it away for the foundation," Barbara replied vaguely.

"I don't mean money. I mean you. They won't listen to you in the boardroom as easily from now on, will they?"

Barbara sighed. "I suppose there will be some reluctance to overcome in the future," she said slowly. "But if I had it all to do over, I'd still back the Thirty-seventh Street Center. Somebody has to keep pushing or the

Calvin Foundation will grind to a complete halt. It will become a dinosaur.''

''Well, I'm going home for the afternoon,'' Brad announced. ''I'll see you when you get back.''

When Brad was gone, Barbara finished tidying her office and went out into the dance studio. The sound of her footsteps echoed through the room, and she stopped to take one more look around, as if this would be the last time she would see the Thirty-seventh Street Center. Looking around at the floor-to-ceiling mirror, the brightly-painted plasterboard, and the polished wood floor, she remembered the day when she and Brad had first walked into this place. They had encountered nothing but heaps of trash, cracked, peeling walls, and a bare bulb hanging on a dusty cord. But Brad had announced that this was it—the place they were looking for. It had only been a few months, but what a difference they had made. Barbara felt a lump in her throat when she thought about the trash piling up again on the clean, polished floor, and the mirrors shattering, and the paint peeling off the walls. In another year, it would be as if the Center had never existed. Unable to bear these visions any longer, Barbara hurried out the front door and locked it behind her.

Bogey danced with joy when he saw Morgan standing in the hall as Barbara opened the door. Morgan bent over and scooped up the little dog, tucking him under one arm. ''Here, let me carry that,'' he said cheerfully, reaching for her suitcase.

''That's all right, I've got it,'' Barbara replied flatly.

Morgan stopped and looked at Barbara closely. ''You sound like I'm taking you to the state prison to begin your life sentence,'' he said in a serious voice. ''You don't have to come if you don't want to.''

"No, I think I want to come," Barbara said slowly. "But somehow, this just doesn't feel right. I can't explain it, but if you could have seen Brad this afternoon, or seen the Center . . ."

"We're leaving Brad and the Center here," Morgan said carefully. "If you have anything else to say about them, say it now, because as soon as we leave they're strictly off limits."

"I understand," Barbara replied. "I agree to the ground rules, but I guess I should warn you that I'm not in a very sociable mood tonight. I'm sorry."

"Don't apologize. Real people get to feeling that way sometimes. That rain cloud over your head is going to blow clean away when you see the sunshine on the lake," Morgan said as he placed a gentle kiss on her forehead. Barbara was silent, with Bogey curled up on her lap, as Morgan drove out of the city. The view from the car was uninteresting for the first hour or so as they drove through the continuous cities that lined the southern part of Lake Michigan. Morgan didn't try to make conversation as they drove on after the sun set and Barbara sat absorbed in her own thoughts.

She found herself wondering if this trip was a mistake. She could imagine nothing but awkwardness in the days ahead, since she was barely speaking to the man she was with. It wasn't fair to be so brusque with Morgan, but when she tried to make conversation she found that she couldn't think of anything to say.

The nearly-full moon had risen high overhead when Morgan finally stopped the car. Barbara, lost in her thoughts, was surprised to find that they arrived.

Morgan had pulled up beside a small A-frame cottage that faced a long, gentle slope of sandy beach leading down to the water. Nestled in the depression between two dunes topped with dark fir trees, it looked very cozy and secluded. The beach was an eerie silver in the pale moonlight, and the black water lapped gently against the sand. Barbara got out of the car and looked out over the lake for a long moment. The sky was slightly overcast and few stars showed through, but the moon was surrounded by a bright ring.

"It's going to rain tomorrow," Barbara said softly. "A ring around the moon means rain."

"If it rains, it rains," Morgan replied as he got the luggage out of the trunk. He led the way up the stairs to the second-story entrance and unlocked the sliding glass door that was positioned off the wide redwood deck. Inside, he flipped on the lights and set the bags down in the middle of the living room.

The second floor consisted of one open room that served as living room, dining room, and kitchen. It was finished in varnished pine, with a fieldstone fireplace at one end, and was decorated with rustic but comfortable-looking furniture. The small kitchen area was well equipped with copper-bottomed pans hanging over the stove and a butcher-block counter. A spiral staircase led from the center of the room to the third floor.

"This is very nice," Barbara said awkwardly.

"I built it myself," Morgan replied. "It came in a kit."

Barbara smiled, thinking he was making a joke.

"I'm serious," Morgan said defensively. "I bought it from a company that sells do-it-yourself houses from a catalogue. It came on a railroad flatcar with all the pieces pre-cut and labeled, and a detailed set of instructions. I'd never done anything like this before, but I think it turned out well. I hired a crane for a day to put the A-frame members in place, but I did the rest by myself."

"How long did it take you?" Barbara asked.

"Two years of working most weekends."

As the conversation lagged, Barbara found herself standing in the center of the room not knowing what to say or do. She looked at Morgan for a clue, but found him looking just as lost and awkward.

"I'll take your bags upstairs," Morgan finally said. "I'll sleep on the couch down here, tonight."

Barbara just nodded her assent and followed him up the spiral staircase.

The third floor was a smaller room with walls that slanted in to form the peak of the roof. There was a small balcony that looked out over the lake at one end, and a picture window looking back to the dunes at the other. The floor was covered with a thick braided rug and the bed had a simple patchwork coverlet—spare, but cozy. The simple, unaffected decor of the entire cottage surprised Barbara because it was so different from Morgan's apartment and office in the city.

Morgan noticed her expression as she took in her surroundings. "Not what you expected?" he asked.

"Frankly no," Barbara replied. "It's all so down to earth. Not like your place in town at all."

"Even I like to come back down to earth sometimes."

With that they had reached another impasse, and Morgan shoved his hands into his pockets, looking as if he'd like to say something but lacked the proper words.

"Tomorrow is going to be better," Barbara said softly. "I know that I want to be here, so tomorrow's got to be better."

Morgan smiled wanly and went back down the steps.

Barbara awoke to the smell of bacon and coffee and the sound of rain falling on the roof over her head. Dressing quickly in a pair of white slacks and a pink plaid shirt, she went downstairs to find Morgan hard at work fixing breakfast. He had a plain white apron tied around his waist and was dressed in a pair of faded jeans and a blue chambray work shirt. Barbara had never seen him dressed so casually.

"Good morning," he said cheerfully. "I hope you're hungry."

Barbara was surprised to find that she *was* hungry. Maybe the odor of cooking had stimulated her appetite, or maybe the week of picking at her food had finally caught up with her, but whatever the reason, she was famished. "I think I could eat a horse," she replied sincerely "Why don't you let me finish that?"

"Not on your life," Morgan replied firmly. "You just sit down and get ready to eat. You aren't the only person in the world who knows how to cook." He flashed her a charming smile before scooping scrambled eggs out of the skillet and onto the two plates on the counter. After adding the buttered toast, he poured two cups of coffee. "Oh, almost forgot," he said as he started to put the plates on the table, then went back for the bacon.

"Delicious," Barbara said after sampling the meal. "You have talents I never imagined." Morgan smiled back at her as he started to eat his own breakfast.

"You look wonderful this morning," Morgan said after a while. "Did you sleep well?"

Barbara nodded and went on eating. The morning had brought her a new peace of mind. With the problems of the Center far away in Chicago, being with Morgan was already beginning to seem natural again. Now, as she watched him eat, she couldn't imagine him doing anything that would hurt her or her concerns. She knew she was avoiding the real issues, but now that she was here all the things that had upset her back in Chicago seemed relatively unimportant.

"I'm afraid we may be stranded indoors this morning.

I guess a ring around the moon does mean rain," Morgan said. "It doesn't look like it's going to let up soon, either."

"Mmm. I heard it as soon as I woke up. You know, I think rain on the roof is one of the most beautiful sounds; it's so relaxing. If I hadn't smelled all this good food, I probably would have turned over and gone back to sleep."

When they had finished eating, Morgan cleared the table and Barbara helped him wash the dishes. The conversation stayed light as they both carefully avoided any subject that might bring back the tension between them.

"Now what?" Barbara asked as Morgan put the skillet back on its hook over the stove.

"When I was little, my mother would always get out the coloring books and crayons on rainy days," Morgan said with a chuckle. "But I'm afraid I left my crayons back in the city."

Barbara laughed at the thought of two adults coloring on a rainy morning. "That's all right. I was never very good at staying inside the lines."

"What? Are you actually admitting that you were a failure at something? I'm sorry, I just can't picture it," Morgan said with mock dismay.

"I wouldn't want to color your opinion of me," Barbara said, laughing with him, "but it's absolutely true. I was never any good at coloring books because I always wanted to make my own pictures."

Morgan leaned back against the counter and smiled at Barbara, not saying anything more. After a moment, Barbara started to feel self-conscious under his gaze.

"Is my shirt buttoned the wrong way?" she asked. "You keep staring at me."

"No, you look perfect," he replied softly. "I can't stop

looking at you because I've missed you and it's been too long since I've seen you laugh. I think I'd rather see you smile than the sunshine." Reaching out, he took her hand and led Barbara to the sofa. "I'll tell you what you're supposed to do on rainy days. You're supposed to sit here and watch the rain come down." He put an arm around Barbara's shoulders and they sat together watching the raindrops splash on the deck outside the sliding glass door. Beyond the wet sand of the beach, the lake was a dark gray that bled into the lighter gray of the sky at the horizon. There was almost no wind, so the rain fell straight down, gently but persistently soaking the landscape. The gloomy weather only made the cottage seem warmer and cozier.

Barbara laid her head on Morgan's shoulder and sighed. "You're right," she said softly. "This beats coloring any day."

"Didn't I tell you that everything would be all right when we got away from Chicago?"

Barbara nodded. But his remark reminded her of the conflicts she had left behind, and it tainted the warm atmosphere. "You know, this doesn't change anything," she said sadly.

"Shh, none of that," Morgan chided quietly. "No shoptalk allowed."

"I know, but not talking about our problem isn't going to make it go away, Morgan. I could sit here with you for a year, but as soon as we go back to Chicago the same problems are going to be waiting for us."

"I hope that by the time we get back to Chicago you'll see how unimportant those problems are."

"They look unimportant from here, especially when you hold me this way. But the fact remains that your life's work and mine are in conflict, and I don't see any way to resolve that," Barbara replied seriously.

"All right," Morgan said gently. "I'll be the first one to break the rule and say the forbidden words. The Thirty-seventh Street Center isn't your life's work. It is just one of many projects you've worked on and will work on. For that matter, the industrial park is just one thing I've worked on. You see? By January we'll hardly remember either one."

"The Center is just one project I've worked on, but it's far from insignificant. It's what brought me here. Without the Center I would never have met you. And when my involvement in the Center is finished, it will be time for me to go back to New York—whether the Center is a success or not."

"You can't be talking about leaving Chicago—not yet." Morgan's voice was tinged with distress.

"Sooner or later, I'll have to," Barbara replied. "You knew that from the start."

"Somehow, I thought you'd want to stay around," Morgan replied, sounding slightly hurt. "You mean a great deal to me, Barbara, and I hope I mean something to you."

"You do, Morgan, but that doesn't change the basic facts. We've shared something very special because we happened to be going in the same direction for a while, but the time is coming when our paths are going to part. We've both got our careers, and—"

"Barbara, I know I said I'm satisfied with my life the way it is, but I'm not so sure about that anymore. I don't want things to go on the way they are. I want things that bachelors don't have, like children and a real home and the security of knowing that the same woman is going to be waiting for me every night when I come home."

"Is that a proposal of marriage?" Barbara asked, sitting up to look directly at Morgan. His expression was as sincere as his words.

"I don't want to tie you down to that right now,' Morgan said carefully. "The time isn't right. The next few months are going to be really hectic and I couldn't ask you to give up everything in your life to follow me through that craziness. But I don't want to lose you either. I guess I'm asking you to be patient and hold on for a little while."

"What craziness?" Barbara asked. "Your reelection is practically a moot point. Not that it really matters—I can't stay in Chicago indefinitely. Sooner or later I've got to go back to New York."

"Do you? Barbara, I want you to think about this very carefully: I'm not going to run for city council again. When I get back to Chicago next Monday, I'm going to announce my bid for Congress."

"*What?*" Barbara exclaimed. "It's only three months until November."

"The election isn't until next year, but I'll have to win the primary next spring to get on the ballot. I'm well known in Chicago, but the congressional district extends out of the city. In fact, most of it is out in the suburbs and country, where I'll have to start from scratch."

"Then you're going to be leaving Chicago, too," Barbara said slowly.

"Exactly. That's why I say that all this business about the Center and the industrial park is unimportant. Barbara, I'm going to Washington, and I want you to come with me."

# Chapter Nine

"I don't understand." Barbara looked directly at Morgan. "You want me to come to Washington with you, but you don't want to get married right away. What are you proposing?"

"Try to understand. This isn't the right time for us to get married. If you thought I was living in a goldfish bowl before, you haven't seen anything. As soon as I announce my candidacy, I won't have a moment to myself. Every move I make will be open for public scrutiny. That's hardly the way to spend a honeymoon, Barbara. And assuming that I'm elected, life in Washington is going to be a whole new experience. I don't have any right to ask you to take on anything as demanding as being a congressman's wife without time to acclimate yourself."

"If I wanted to marry you, I'd want to share your life," Barbara said carefully.

"You don't know what you're saying, Barbara. If I win the election, I'll go to Washington and spend the next

133

year getting established, then it will be time to talk about getting married. In the meantime, we can still see each other. New York is a lot closer to Washington than Chicago is. You'll be able to see how things are before you make up your mind about marrying me."

"And what if you lose?"

Morgan smiled his most charming and confident smile. "Me? Lose?" he said with a chuckle.

"Excuse me," Barbara laughingly replied before she became serious again. "But none of this changes the basic problem, Morgan—what about the Center? Just because you're planning to leave Chicago doesn't mean that nothing there matters anymore. If the Center fails, it will have effects on more than just the Thirty-seventh Street neighborhood. It was an experiment, a test case for the Calvin Foundation. If the Center fizzles out, the Calvin Foundation will never fund that type of project again. That won't be forgotten by January. I think what we're doing at the Center is important, and I've staked a great deal of my career on its success."

"As we sit here, I can't do anything about the Center," Morgan said sincerely. "All I can do is ask you to trust that I'll look for a solution that will make everybody as happy as possible. I can't promise that I'll accomplish anything, and I certainly can't propose that the council change the whole industrial park because my lady doesn't like what we've done, but there are always options. Maybe I can find one that will keep the Center from becoming a complete loss."

"Why?" Barbara asked, feeling slightly vexed. "So I'll be grateful? So I won't be mad at you anymore? Is that how you look after the interests of the city at large?" It was almost as if he were condescending to save her project. Barbara didn't want him to save the Center just because it was her project; she wanted it to succeed on its own merit.

"Which side are you on?" Morgan replied with a sigh. "Look, let's not talk about it anymore. As I said, we can't do anything about it from here, so talking about it is pointless. I want to talk about us—about all the years we're going to spend together and all the wonderful times we'll have."

"Morgan, I'm not sure we have any future," Barbara replied slowly, "but I do know I'm glad I'm here with you right now, and I don't want to spoil it with useless arguing any more than you do." She put her head back on his shoulder and let the tension flow out of her body. Her worries about the Center slipped away as she let the sound of rain on the roof fill her ears. All she wanted was to enjoy her time here. When this week was over she could go back and let her career become the center of her life once more, but for these few days she would live for the moment and not the future.

The rain soon cleared, the clouds parted, and the sun shone down on the beach. After lunch, Morgan and Barbara went down to the lake and walked barefoot along the damp, sparkling sand, letting the waves erase their footprints behind them. The sand was cool and soft underfoot, and the air was warm and clean from the rain. Morgan found several flat, rounded stones and threw them sidearm out over the water, making them skip three or four times before they disappeared under the waves. Bogey scampered along at their feet, playing tag with the waves and barking with excitement when the water washed over his little paws. At one spot he stopped and dug frantically in the sand only to be totally perplexed when his hole filled with water.

A short way down the beach from the cottage, they came across a little boy and girl building a castle in the sand. Morgan stopped to admire the structure but Bogey came running up and dove right into the middle, knocking down more than half the castle and startling the children into laughter.

"Bogey!" Barbara cried. "How could you?" She reached down to scoop him up and scold him, but the dog jumped back out of her reach. Despite the destruction of their castle, the children were enchanted with Bogey. They laughed even harder when the little dog made a strafing run and snatched their red plastic sand shovel, carrying it a few yards off and crouching down with the toy between his front paws. "You give that back, right now," Barbara said sternly. Bogey wagged his tail and carried the shovel back to the children, obediently dropping it down in the little boy's lap.

Morgan laughed at Bogey's antics. "He likes an audience better than I do," he said. Bogey sat up and begged for the children then pretended to fall over with a startled bark. The boy and girl laughed and applauded his performance.

"Come on, Bogey," Barbara said, starting off down the beach. "Let the kids rebuild their castle." Bogey barked farewell to his audience and came to Barbara's heel.

"I never realized what a little ham that dog is," Morgan commented as they walked on, hand in hand.

"You have to be careful not to encourage him too much," Barbara replied knowingly. "He'll keep up the cute routine until everybody is bored to tears."

After a long walk on the beach, Barbara and Morgan returned to the cottage then went into town to buy groceries for the remainder of the week. When they had returned and all the supplies were put away, Morgan suggested that they change into their bathing suits and go for a swim.

Barbara put on her simple navy blue bikini and picked up a bottle of suntan lotion. She had had little opportunity to go out in the sun this summer and her skin was very pale in contrast to the dark-colored bathing suit. Even though it was fairly late in the afternoon, she decided that a sunscreen would be necessary to prevent a burn. She quickly smoothed the lotion over her legs, arms, and stomach, then went down the stairs to find Morgan.

"Could you put some of this on my back?" she asked, handing him the bottle.

"With pleasure," he replied with a smile. A shiver went down her spine as his hand smoothed the cool lotion over her back. His fingers lingered on the graceful curve of her waist and then came back up to caress her shoulders and the nape of her neck.

Barbara turned around to face him, taking a long look at the firm muscles of his chest and the broad expanse of his shoulders that tapered down to a trim waist and taut abdomen. The life of a city councilman had done nothing to make Morgan flabby or slack. Barbara chuckled as a silly thought came to her head.

"What's so funny?" Morgan asked defensively. "Have you any idea how psychologically damaging it is to have a woman laugh at you when you put on a bathing suit?"

"Believe me, I wasn't laughing at you. I was just thinking what a shame it is that they don't have a bathing suit competition in congressional elections. You'd be a shoo-in."

"I'll keep that in mind," Morgan joked. "Do you think I could get the feminist vote that way?"

"Depends on what the opposition looks like," Barbara replied thoughtfully.

"Come on," Morgan said with a laugh as he took her

hand, "let's get into the water before I decide to drow
you."

The lake was chilly, and as they waded in, Barbar
could feel goose bumps rising on her arms from th
cold. She hesitated for a moment then took a dee
breath and dove in the rest of the way. After swimmin
a few strokes out toward deeper water, she relaxed an
floated on her back, letting the sun warm her chest an
legs. She looked up at the clear, blue sky and sculle
lightly with her fingertips to maintain her position. Th
waves rocked her gently, and she let her mind dri
without any conscious thoughts or purpose. She migh
have drifted indefinitely but for the cold water that sud
denly dripped onto her warm stomach.

"Hey!" she cried, thrashing and putting her fee
down to find herself in shoulder-deep water. "What di
you do that for?" Morgan had poured a handful of lak
water on her and was quickly swimming away. Barbar
launched herself after him and caught up in the kne
deep water near the beach. She reached down an
picked up a handful of wet sand from the bottom, the
slapped it against the back of his bathing trunks. Sh
turned to make her own getaway, but Morgan was to
fast for her. He reached down and grabbed her ankl
yanking her off her feet and causing a splash as Barbar
hit the surface of the water. Barbara recovered an
stood up with mock dignity.

"You, sir, are no gentleman," she said pompously
She started to stalk away toward the beach but turne
suddenly and slapped the surface of the water wit
both arms, throwing up a wave that hit Morgan from th
waterline to the top of his head. In another momen
they were both churning the water, each attempting t
throw up a larger splash.

"Truce!" Morgan cried out at last. "If we keep this u

ve're going to create a tidal wave that will wipe out cot-
ages as far north as Traverse City."

"Oh, what's the matter? Can't take it?" Barbara said
vith a helpless giggle. She walked out of the water and
eturned to the beach where she sat down on the warm
.lanket. Morgan came and sat down next to her. Beads
.f water gleamed on his shoulders, and his short hair
vas plastered to his head. Barbara shook out her own
.urls and reached for the suntan lotion to replace what
he water had washed off, lying down on her stomach
vhile Morgan put more lotion on her back. The sensa-
ion of his fingers sliding over her damp skin was won-
lerfully relaxing.

"What shall we have for supper?" Morgan asked as he
ay down beside Barbara.

"Hmmm, something terribly elegant and complicated
ike . . . hot dogs and marshmallows," Barbara replied
azily.

"A great idea. We can build a fire and roast them right
.ere."

Barbara put her head down and dozed in the warm,
oft sand as Morgan got up to gather driftwood for a fire.
`he sun was sinking toward the surface of the lake
vhen she woke and found Morgan tending a small fire
.f twigs and driftwood just a few feet away. He had
.rought down the food from the cottage and was using a
mall knife to strip the bark from a green stick to use as a
:ooking fork. Barbara sat up and brushed the hair out of
.er face.

"I didn't mean for you to do all the work," Barbara
aid apologetically. "You shouldn't have let me sleep so
ong."

"What work? Bringing down the hot dogs and
:etchup?"

"Give me that and I'll show you how a French-trained

cook roasts a hot dog," Barbara said playfully. She skewered the hot dog and held it over the fire. "The technique is very important."

"Is it?" Morgan asked with a chuckle. "I suppose it's important to get just the right amount of sand sprinkled onto it?"

"Of course," Barbara replied. Morgan put his own hot dog on the end of a second stick and held it over the fire. After a few moments, he produced two rolls, ketchup, mustard, and two paper plates. When they had finished eating, they watched their plates burn in the small fire.

The setting sun turned the water to orange fire and etched a golden rim around the few small clouds in the western sky. When a cool breeze started to blow off the water, Morgan went back to the cottage and returned with another blanket. He wrapped it around them as they sat in silence on the beach and watched the sun slip beneath the surface of the lake.

As the last daylight faded in a rosy glow on the horizon, the first stars winked in the darkening sky. The transition from day to night cast a spell that was as mesmerizing as the beauty they found in one another's arms. Barbara felt as secure and protected as she had ever felt in her life, and she let her head rest against Morgan's warm, sturdy shoulder, listening to the soft sound of his breathing and the gentle lapping of the waves.

"What did you mean when you said you weren't sure we had any future together?" Morgan asked softly when the darkness had enveloped them.

"I don't know. I don't want to think about the future. I just want to be with you here and now," she replied.

"I want to think about the future. Barbara, I love you.

want to know that we're going to be together for the rest of our lives."

"But you don't want to get married right away . . ."

"Not right away, but eventually," Morgan replied defensively.

"Don't you see? If you really wanted to get married you'd be setting a date—after the election, if that's so important—but you'd be tying it down. You're not sure, Morgan. Just like me, you've been on your own so long that you can't really imagine changing. You say you don't want to tie me down, but you're really afraid of making a commitment you'd have to break later."

"What about you? Are you ready to make a commitment?" he asked gently.

"I love you. As we sit here like this, all that nonsense about the Center doesn't matter. I just want to be with you, like this forever. But we can't sit on a beach for the rest of our lives, and that's where the trouble starts. I just can't tell what's going to happen when we go back to the city. I'm not saying that my love for you hinges on whether or not the Center survives. I'm just afraid that when we're faced with all the practical things, we're going to start longing for our old, safe, independent lifestyles."

"We can work it out," Morgan answered. "We'll just take our time. I'll be the only congressman in Washington who spends all his weekends in New York. And when the time comes when we're both sure, and I know that time will come, we'll get married."

The full moon was rising in the sky behind them and its pale light turned the sand to powdery silver, glinting off the waves in shimmering patterns. The stars shone brighter than Barbara had ever seen them, and the fleeting trail of a shooting star caught her eye as it fell toward the dark surface of the lake.

"Make a wish," Barbara said softly as the trail faded from the sky.

"What did you wish for?" Morgan whispered next to her ear.

Barbara hesitated, unable to give words to the wish that had formed in her mind. As much as she loved Morgan, she had found herself wishing that he would lose the upcoming primary. As a city councilman, Morgan found it difficult to save very much of himself for a personal life. How much less of him would be left for her if he were in Congress? The more she imagined what was to come, the more she saw him slipping away from her if his ambitions were satisfied. His work would always come first because it was important and had to be done, and because Morgan Newman couldn't live outside the spotlight of public attention.

That simple truth was clear to her here, far from the crowds and reporters and television cameras. There was a private man who lived inside the public façade, but the private Morgan Newman was much too delicate and subtle to stand by himself without the protection of the slick, showy public image. The private Morgan Newman was a man of simple tastes and quiet words. The public Morgan Newman was an ego without substance. Combined, they made the perfect politician—a conscience with the skill to make his principles into realities. Without the showy front, he wouldn't be able to accomplish his goals; without the virtues of his inner self, he would be just one more shifty politician.

But the perfect politician couldn't be the perfect lover. As long as he dedicated himself to the public good, there would never be enough left over for Barbara

Danbury. If she was to love this man, she would have to love the politician as well, because the public image was as much a part of his reality as the face he showed when they were alone together. Barbara knew that Congress was the next logical step for Morgan, and he needed the office as much as he needed her. But a small spot of selfishness made her wish that his ambitions would elude him. Somehow, she knew she could find a way to be the councilman's woman, but how could she compete with the demands of Congress and the nation?

"You haven't answered me," Morgan said softly. "You have to tell—there can be no secrets between true lovers."

"I wished for more time to have you to myself," Barbara replied half truthfully. "I'm going to miss you so much when you're off campaigning. What did you wish for?"

"Guess," Morgan answered as he drew her closer and smoothly unfastened the top of her bathing suit. He gently lowered her down until she was lying on the soft blanket.

Barbara let out a low laugh as he pushed aside her bathing suit to hold the full swell of her breast in his hand and brought his face to hers in a warm, tender kiss. "Your wish is a lot easier to fill than mine," Barbara whispered as she ran her fingers through his hair and let her hands wander to his strong shoulders.

"It was more than just making love to you," Morgan replied as his lips explored the smooth skin of her neck and his fingers teased her sensitive curves with small, feathery touches. "If I had my wish, I would never let you go."

Barbara's heart pounded as the undeniable sensations grew within her. The bottom half of her bathing suit soon followed the top, and she luxuriated in the sensation of Morgan's warm, bare skin against her own. Her body told her that any estrangement that had come between them was gone; she experienced his touch as if she had never felt it before. The intensity of the feelings that he coaxed from her with his gentle stroking robbed her of all reason. No thought guided her hands as they grasped the firm contours of Morgan's back and pulled him closer to mold together every curve of their bodies. She belonged to him wholeheartedly and wanted nothing more than to satisfy him and be satisfied. There was no more to the universe than the man who surrounded, covered, and penetrated her.

Even as Barbara moved toward the wonderful, sweet moment of release, Morgan relaxed and held her back. "slowly, my love," he whispered in her ear. "We have all the time in the world." Setting a slower tempo, he teased her, using his caresses to fan her desire to a point where she thought she could bear it no longer, then calming her only to excite her again.

Then, when the passion within her could be contained no longer and her body trembled with a need that seemed almost agonizing in its intensity, she found the satisfaction that she longed for as waves of fulfillment washed through every fiber of her body. A deep moan escaped Morgan's lips as he joined her in the climax of their shared love.

They lay cradled in one another's arms and heard the sounds of the water and the night once more. Morgan's body was pleasantly warm and damp as he rested against Barbara. She sighed and nuzzled against his neck, feeling a sweet sleepiness creep over her.

"Don't go to sleep, love," Morgan whispered in Barbara's ear just as she started to drift off.

"Why not?" Barbara mumbled.

"Because I'm not through with you yet," he replied.

"I'm too tired," Barbara protested.

"I know just what will wake you up," Morgan said. He kissed her soundly then jumped to his feet and yanked the blankets away.

"Hey!" Barbara cried, sitting up with a start. "That's not nice."

Morgan reached down and pulled her to her feet. A cool breeze played over her body and she was suddenly embarrassed to be standing naked on the beach, even though there was no one but Morgan to see her and he was wearing no more than she.

"Give me back the blanket," she pleaded, half serious, half laughing.

"Oh, no. If I give you back the blanket you'll just curl up and go to sleep."

Barbara started to look around for her discarded bathing suit, but Morgan beat her to it and snatched it off the sand. He rolled the bathing suit and blanket together and tossed them both as far up the beach as he could. Barbara started after them, but Morgan grabbed her arm and started to drag her toward the water.

"Stop that," Barbara giggled. "I don't want to go back in the water. It'll be too cold. I'll turn blue."

"Sorry about that, you're going anyway."

Morgan pulled her down the beach and they splashed into the cold water, Barbara giggling protests every step of the way. The chill was invigorating, and when they got waist deep Barbara pulled away from Morgan and dove in. She came up a short way off and swam several strokes out into deeper water. When she stopped and looked back, Morgan was swimming to her with powerful strokes that sent up a spray of water that sparkled in the moonlight. Barbara started to swim away from him, but he caught up with her quickly and grabbed her ankle, pulling her to a stop.

"Mmm. I seem to have caught a mermaid," Morgan said as he pulled her in. "I won't let you go until you promise me three wishes."

Barbara put her arms around Morgan's neck and let herself float in the water next to him. "All right, but I warn you, I don't think I could survive three more wishes like the last one."

"Let me see, what can I wish for? How about health, wealth, and happiness?"

"Easier wished for than received," Barbara said softly. "But would you settle for love, loyalty, and friendship?"

Morgan put his hands on her waist and pulled her closer. His body was warm in contrast to the cold water, and Barbara felt a rekindled thrill as she rested against him.

"And would you settle for the imperfect attentions of an imperfect man?"

"Perfection is boring," Barbara replied. "I'll settle for Morgan Newman with all his faults."

"All my faults? Boy you can't leave my ego alone for a minute, can you?" Morgan said with a laugh.

"You should be thankful. Just think of what a pompous fool you'd become if you didn't have me to burst your bubble every once in a while," Barbara teased.

"That's the trouble—I like being a pompous fool," Morgan laughed. "I really can't figure out what I see in you—too tall, too smart for your own good, too beautiful to be real." He punctuated his speech with kisses.

"Too cold to stay out here any longer," Barbara added as her teeth started to chatter. "Last one out of the water is a rotten egg." She pushed away from Morgan to swim toward shore, then ran up the beach to the blanket. She was still shivering when Morgan joined her but he soon made her warm again.

# Chapter Ten

❧

The week at the cottage would always remain in Barbara's memory as a refuge where time stood still, frozen between the troubles she had left behind and the challenges that lay ahead. They spent long lazy afternoons on the beach and enchanted nights in one another's arms. Morgan didn't speak about his upcoming campaign again and Barbara dismissed all thoughts about the Center or the Calvin Foundation.

There was a serenity about the time they spent at the lake that convinced Barbara the problems between her and Morgan could be solved. She finally felt as if she understood the contradictions that made up the man. The politician in him, the part that belonged to the public, was a complex construction of ego and image that served to protect the other persona—the Morgan that belonged exclusively to Barbara.

But the ego and vanity were more than tools for accomplishing his goals. Barbara could see that Morgan needed the limelight. If forced to retire from public life, he would surely perish—in spirit, if nothing else. He needed to move on to the bigger political arena, and Barbara knew that she could never occupy the center stage of his life; his work would always have to come first. At the same time she knew that nothing could come between her and her private Morgan. Barbara made up her mind to accept the reality that she would always occupy a position of secondary importance in his life, because she could see that what he could spare for her came directly from his heart. She came to realize that she would accept whatever Morgan offered her and be grateful for the part she could play in his life, because the simple truth was that she loved him.

They were together all the time during that beautiful week, with the exception of Wednesday afternoon when Morgan suddenly decided he had to go into town to use a telephone.

He refused to take Barbara with him and upon his return wouldn't tell her what he did. Barbara didn't discover what it was all about until she returned to work on Monday.

She walked to the Center with a spring in her step that had been notably missing the week before her vacation. Her own high spirits were easily understandable, but to her surprise, she found Brad in a mood that bordered on drunken revelry. The powerfully-built dancer greeted her at the door with a bear hug that threatened to crush her and a grin that could have lit a dark night.

"What was that for?" Barbara asked in surprise.

"I don't know how you did it, and I don't care, but whatever you did, you're a genius!" Brad beamed.

"What did I do?"

"You got the city council to move the industrial development," Brad replied.

"They moved the industrial development?"

"You didn't know about it?"

"Of course I didn't know about it. I've been out of town all week," Barbara said in surprise. "I didn't have anything to do with it, but I'm delighted—more than delighted!"

"You didn't have anything to do with it? Sure," Brad said knowingly. "They're calling the new plan the Newman Plan, and you've been out of town with Morgan Newman all week."

"How did you know?" Barbara sputtered. "I never told you who I was going away with."

"I'm not stupid," Brad replied with a smile. "After the news broke about the new industrial development, I tried to call the councilman's office to thank him. I found out that he was out of town for the whole week. The new development arrangements were all made by his aides. Now it doesn't take a genius to put together the facts . . ."

"I didn't know anything about it, I swear," Barbara said sincerely. "But, if you've got your mind made up, I'll be glad to take the credit."

Barbara went straight to the telephone in her office and called Morgan.

"Why didn't you tell me what you were doing when you went into town?" she asked as soon as he came on the line.

"I didn't want to get your hopes up if it didn't work out," He replied. "It was very iffy. Everything depended on whether the Amalgamated people would settle for the new site and whether the paperwork had been completed on the original land transfer. It was almost too late to change anything."

"You put everybody to all that trouble just for me?"

"I have you to thank for goading me into giving the whole project more consideration and coming up with a much better solution," Morgan replied. "If this wasn't a better way to go, nobody would have agreed to change the plans."

"How is one site better than the other?" Barbara asked.

"Rather than knocking down a whole neighborhood and building a new factory, the Amalgamated people are going to renovate an old plant that's not in use. It will cost them less money, and nobody is going to be out of a home. They're going to take over the old United Tire plant on the southside—it fits their needs perfectly. I feel like a fool for not thinking of it earlier. The council just got into a rut, thinking that we had to knock something down to build this new factory."

"Oh, dear," Barbara said with a little giggle. "Brad thinks I slept with you to get you to change the plans."

"Well, didn't you?" Morgan said mischievously.

"You'd better know better than that," Barbara replied gravely.

"I do know better than that—that's why I didn't tell you what I was doing. Now, you better let me get back to work. I've got press conference in fifteen minutes to announce my candidacy for Congress. Wish me luck."

"You don't need any luck," Barbara said with a laugh. "Your opponent is the one who's going to need the luck."

"Then say you love me."

"I love you," Barbara said softly.

"With that kind of backing, I could run for king," Morgan replied.

Barbara hurried home at noon to watch the videotape of Morgan's press conference on the news. She settled down in front of the television with a tuna sandwich just as Morgan came on camera and read a short statement announcing his intentions. Barbara felt a small flush of pride as John Donaldson, the incumbent congressman who was abandoning his office because of health problems, stood up and endorsed Morgan's candidacy. After the preliminary statements had been delivered, Morgan calmly answered the reporters' questions and laid out the basic platform of his campaign. For once, Barbara listened intently to every word he said and even made a mental note to question him on a point or two the next time they talked—to show him that she cared and was paying attention.

She felt a kind of excitement about this new campaign that she couldn't entirely explain. Just a few days ago Barbara had been afraid that Congress would take Morgan farther away from her. But now, as she watched Morgan start off his campaign, she felt as if she were a part of what was going to happen. For the first time, it occurred to her that she could spend more time with Morgan and have more of him for herself if she were to make herself a part of the political world that he was so involved in. It was such a simple idea she wondered that she hadn't thought of it before. She didn't have to keep herself separate from Morgan's work. She could work with him, and the Calvin Foundation could survive without her for a while. Barbara was suddenly elated at the prospect of joining Morgan's campaign in any capacity that she could.

Sensing her excitement, Bogey jumped up on the sofa beside Barbara. She picked him up and held him out in front of her to look into his black, sparkling eyes. "How would you like to be the world's first campaign dog?" she asked with a giggle. "You'd just love to kiss the babies, wouldn't you?"

She told her plan to Morgan that night, but was surprised and a little bit hurt when he didn't share her enthusiasm.

"I don't think you should put all your eggs in one basket," he said, dousing her enthusiasm immediately. "You're just getting carried away with the idea of beginning a new project. You don't want to give up your career this soon, do you? It just isn't time for you, yet."

"I thought you'd want me with you," Barbara said, unable to disguise the hurt in her voice.

"I'd like nothing better, but I don't think it would be good for us. Campaigning burns people out, love. I've known couples with very strong marriages who broke up because of the stress of a campaign. I don't want to ruin everything we have because we were too impatient to wait until the time was right."

Barbara accepted Morgan's words, swallowing her disappointment. Very well, she told herself, I can wait.

In the following weeks, she learned the true meaning of waiting. As the dog days of August settled over the city, Morgan's campaign shifted into high gear and he was constantly on the road speaking to various organizations and community gatherings. Ron Caldwell made most of the arrangements, and Morgan had nothing but praise for Ron's ability to coordinate the campaign and get Morgan's name and face into every household in the district. Ron was in his element when it came to strategy and scheduling appearances, but Barbara eventually realized that he was a bit too aggressive and might be overexposing his candidate too early in the game. She kept her opinion of the campaign aide to herself, however, since Morgan relied so heavily on Caldwell.

She considered herself fortunate if she got to spend one evening a week with Morgan. More often than not, Ron would call to cancel Morgan's date because some unexpected opportunity had come up. And the continuous stream of engagements often left him too exhausted to be good company when he did find time for Barbara.

By the end of the first month of the campaign, Barbara began to worry that stress might be taking more out of Morgan than he realized. As they sat on the balcony of his apartment one evening, she was upset to see the weariness in his posture and appearance; Morgan seemed to have aged years in a single month. In public he maintained his vigorous image, but now, as he relaxed, he seemed to sag with the weight of his undertaking.

"You're looking at me the way my mother always did when I had the flu," Morgan said when he noticed Barbara's scrutiny.

"You look so tired, Morgan. You need to rest more," Barbara replied solicitously.

"I can rest after the primary," he said with a yawn. "Except, then I have to start campaigning for the November election."

"What good will winning the election be if you ruin your health along the way?" Barbara asked with a frown.

"Do I look that bad? Is rigor mortis beginning to set in?"

"You look like you're using up all your reserves," Barbara said seriously. "You should take a couple of days off."

"Wouldn't you like that," Morgan said impishly. "Well, I'll show you something, lady. I've got reserves that you don't even know about." Morgan jumped out of his chair and picked Barbara up in a smooth swoop. "We'll just see who's all tuckered out," he said huskily as he carried her inside.

When Septemper took the majority of the Center's

students back to school Brad rearranged the schedules to concentrate on evening and weekend classes. Barbara knew she was staying at the Center longer than was necessary; the time had finally come when Brad could handle things by himself. Through the fall, winter, and spring, the workload would be reduced, and by next summer Brad would be able to hire an assistant to do the things Barbara was still doing.

She had been delaying her departure for the obvious reason of staying near Morgan. But in the second week of September events took a turn that convinced her to make plans to leave as soon as possible.

It was a warm Wednesday afternoon when she started to clean out her desk at the Center and arrange the files and records so they could be taken over by someone else. She worked quickly, with a grim determination to get this part of her departure over with as fast as she could. She hardly noticed as she worked that she was slamming file drawers and cabinet doors, and she hadn't been at it long when Brad came into her office to see what she was doing. He carried his lunch of fish and chips with him and set it down in the center of Barbara's desk, then stood back with his hands on his hips.

"What's going on here?" he asked after a few moments.

Barbara stopped unloading the file drawer she was working on and turned to face him. Catching sight of the greasy cardboard container of fish on her desk, she eyed it with disgust as she felt her stomach turn over.

"Would you mind taking that garbage out of here?" she asked in an irritated voice.

Brad picked up the fish and gave Barbara a strange look. "That's good fish from the Capt'n's Place," he said in an odd tone of voice. "I thought you loved fish and chips."

"There must be something wrong with you if you can eat that," Barbara replied, turning back to the filing cabinet. "It smells like it's been out of the water for about three weeks."

"Never mind my lunch," Brad said suspiciously. "I want to know what you're doing."

"What does it look like?" Barbara snapped, slamming the drawer shut. "I'm packing up to leave."

"Why?"

"You know perfectly well why."

"Yes, I think I do," Brad said in a calm tone of voice.

"What do you mean by that?" Barbara asked in a voice perilously close to tears.

"I grew up with three older sisters," Brad replied carefully. "I think I recognize the signs."

"Don't talk nonsense," Barbara retorted, desperately trying to keep Brad from saying what they both knew. "I'm getting ready to leave because it's time. My involvement with the Center was always meant to be temporary. You insisted on that, as I remember."

"That's true. But if it's honesty time, I could have taken over six weeks ago. You weren't in such a hurry then."

"I hung around longer than I should have." The words dropped out of Barbara's mouth like stones. She knew she wasn't fooling Brad.

"I'll tell you why you're suddenly packing to leave. For the past month you've been running out of the room every time anyone brings in food with a strong odor. You've started having a banana milkshake for lunch every day—something you never particularly liked before. This morning you came to work late because you went to see the doctor. Do I have to complete the riddle?"

Barbara sat down behind her desk and buried her face in her hands, fighting the tears.

"Barbara, I'm your friend. You don't have to run away from your friends," Brad said gently.

"I'm not running away from you," Barbara replied as the first of a flood of tears spilled down her cheek.

"No, you're running away from the S.O.B. that did this to you," Brad said darkly.

Barbara looked up in surprise at the acid in Brad's tone. "Don't be so Victorion," she said. "Nobody 'did' this to me. I was a willing participant."

"But he's not living up to his obligations, is he?" Brad asked.

"It all depends on what you call his obligations," Barbara said evasively. "This is the twentieth century, Brad. I really don't need you to call the bounder out for a duel."

"What are you going to do, slink off to New York to hide your shame?" Brad asked sarcastically. "You're carrying his child, Barbara. He has an obligation to share that responsibility." Brad glared at Barbara and she felt like shrinking away from his anger. His eyes accused her of cowardice, and she wasn't sure she had a defense against the charge.

"I'm not Morgan's only obligation," Barbara said in a weak voice.

"If he was half a man, he wouldn't run out on you now," Brad retorted. "I've known all along that Morgan Newman was a sleazy character."

"I'm the one who's running out," Barbara said guiltily.

"If I get my hands on that slimy—"

"That's enough, Brad," Barbara interrupted sharply. "You're not my father or my older brother, and you're not responsible for defending my honor. I don't need a man to protect me—from anything. I can take care of myself and my child. And that's exactly what I'm going to do when I get back to New York." Barbara's cheeks burned with hot tears. "And get this stinking garbage out of my office before I throw up," she added pointing at the offending fish and chips.

Brad picked up the food and left her office without a word. After she heard him slam the front door, Barbara let her face fall back into her hands and sobbed.

When she finally got home, she sat down at the kitchen table and struggled to regain her composure. She couldn't afford to let herself fall to pieces this way. In the coming months she would need all the self-reliance she could muster. She felt terrible about her argument with Brad. He'd only been trying to offer his help and support, and he didn't deserve the angry things she had said. But the words had tumbled out of their own accord as she hid the truth from him. Brad's accusations against Morgan were completely unfounded, Morgan hadn't refused to honor his obligations—he didn't know she was pregnant. And if Barbara had her way, he wouldn't find out.

As she put on a kettle to make a pot of herb tea, she returned her thoughts to the plans she had been formulating since the doctor had given her the news that morning. She would return to New York as quickly as possible, so that Morgan wouldn't find out about her condition the way Brad had. Morgan's campaign schedule would probably keep him away from her for the remainder of the pregnancy. If he demanded to know why she was leaving, she would tell him that she was breaking off the relationship because of the way he was neglecting her for the campaign.

Barbara let herself feel noble for the sacrifice she was making. She would give up the man she loved for the good of his career. If he found out, Barbara knew he would want to marry her immediately, but she wasn't about to add the extra burdens of a wife and child to Morgan's already stressful life. He had told her that this wasn't the time to get married, so she would keep the truth from him. She might be losing the man she loved, but at least she would have their child to remind her of the love she had known.

The doorbell startled Barbara out of her melodramatic reverie. When she opened the door, she found Morgan pacing in the hall with a dark expression on his face.

"I want to know what's going on, Barbara, right now!" he exclaimed ominously.

"I don't know what you mean," Barbara replied, trying to calm her pounding heart.

"I canceled a very important speaking engagement to come over here," he replied, "so I don't feel like playing games."

"What are you talking about?" Barbara asked innocently.

"You know, Barbara, in all the time we've been together, I've never really had the opportunity to meet and talk to your friend Brad—until this afternoon, that is. I've discovered that he's a thoroughly unpleasant person."

Barbara felt as if her stomach had dropped several feet. Her secret was out and there was no escaping it now. She turned away from Morgan to hide her face, but he took her by the shoulders and turned her around to face him.

"I really don't appreciate finding out that I'm going to be a father by having an enraged stranger come to my office to threaten me." He looked directly at Barbara and waited for an explanation.

"I'm sorry," Barbara mumbled with her eyes cast down. "I wish that hadn't happened. Brad doesn't understand. He's a little overprotective of me sometimes."

"I don't understand either," Morgan said with a frown. "Didn't you think I had a right to know? What's this foolishness about packing up to go back to New York?"

"I wasn't sure myself until this morning," Barbara said lamely.

"But you weren't going to tell me, were you?" Barbara didn't answer and Morgan looked as if he were going to shake her in frustration. "Answer me!" he said angrily.

Barbara shook her head.

"Oh, that's just great," Morgan said bitterly as he let go of her shoulders. "Which adolescent fantasy can I put this down to? I suppose you were going to martyr yourself to save me from the shame of having fathered an illegitimate child. Really, Barbara, you must have been reading Emily Brontë. Maybe you could throw yourself off the roof of a burning building for a big finish."

Barbara gathered her courage and turned to face Morgan. "I don't have to listen to this," she snapped. "You can be civil or you can get out!"

Morgan took a moment to get control of his voice before he spoke again. "Why weren't you going to tell me?" he asked in a more normal tone of voice.

Barbara let out a deep sigh and sat down in a chair. "Because of what you're going to say next," she replied calmly as he sat on the sofa opposite her.

"You're psychic? You know what I'm going to say next?" There was a note of sarcasm in his voice, but Barbara ignored it.

"I don't need to be a psychic to know that you're

going to insist that we get married right away," she said
with a frown.

"Of course I am," Morgan replied. "What else do two
people do in this situation?"

"I don't want to get married because I 'have to.' I don't
have to. I am perfectly capable of supporting myself and
this child."

"You don't have the right," Morgan said. "That child
is as much mine as yours and you can't shut me away
from him."

"I won't try to stop you from seeing him—or her,"
Barbara said flatly, staring at a spot on the floor halfway
between them.

"Why are you talking as if we were working out a sep-
aration agreement with visitation rights?" Morgan
asked in a baffled voice. "I *want* to marry you. I've said
that before now. I love you and I thought you felt the
same way."

"You said you wanted to marry me, but not right
now. You said it wasn't time for me yet. You said that
you didn't want to get married during the campaign,"
Barbara replied.

"I know what I said, but this changes all that. And
just because we get married doesn't mean you have to
join the campaign. You'll need to take care of yourself."

"My pregnancy changes nothing," Barbara retorted
bitterly. "You still don't want me messing around in
your campaign. You want to do 'the right thing.' This
proposal of marriage has nothing to do with love or
with me for that matter. You just want to fulfill your
obligations as you see them. Well I don't want that kind
of marriage!"

"Barbara, you don't understand," Morgan said in a
voice filled with agony. "You think I want to shut you
out of my campaign, but it's not true. I'm trying to pro-

tect you from it. The only kind of marriage I'm offering you is one to a man who loves you so much it hurts. It won't be easy with the campaign going on, but it doesn't matter if this is the right time or not. I want to marry you because for the first time in my life I've found a woman that I love enough to want to spend the rest of my life with."

"You say that tonight, but will you feel the same way when you've had some time to think about it?" Barbara asked warily.

"I don't need time to think about it. I'm as sure as I've ever been about anything in my life."

"I don't doubt that you think you're sure," Barbara said evenly. "You're used to making snap decisions on important matters. But this is too important for a snap decision, Morgan—too important to me, anyway. This isn't a city council ordinance—it's our lives. I want to be your wife more than anything in the world, but I don't want to be the final burden that saps your remaining strength and I don't want to be a noble commitment that you bear like a martyr. I don't want to settle this on the spur of the moment."

"Barbara, I'm not going to feel any different about this next week or next year, but if it will help you to trust me I'll wait—for a few days. I'll wait until Saturday, then we'll talk about it again and start making our wedding plans," Morgan replied firmly.

"It isn't any use if you've already made up your mind," Barbara said with a faint smile. "Promise me that you'll really think about it and take everything into consideration."

"I'll promise anything you want, if you'll promise to marry me when I come back."

Barbara felt a great weight lifting from her shoulders. She could even feel a little bit foolish about her own actions now. Smiling at Morgan she shook her head. "You're impossible," she said softly, "but I think I'm glad that you are."

Morgan stood up and came over to Barbara, pulling her gently to her feet and taking her in his arms. "When?" he whispered in her ear as he held her closer and smoothed his hand through her hair.

"I'm due in April."

"Oh, Barbara." There was awe in Morgan's voice. Then he held her silently for a long time as they savored the peace and beauty that surrounded them. Finally, Morgan spoke softly.

"I'm going to leave now." He kissed her lightly. "And I'm not going to call you or try to see you until Saturday. I'll do exactly as you've asked and give our marriage serious consideration, but don't you dare start worrying about anything. And don't you dare start packing to leave. I'm not going to change my mind. We're going to the courthouse to apply for a marriage license Saturday morning."

# Chapter Eleven

Barbara forgave Brad for confronting Morgan for she realized that his interference had saved her from making a terrible mistake. She returned to the Center the next morning filled with a bright hope for her future and spent the morning unpacking the things she had removed from her desk, humming away cheerfully. Her only regret was that Brad and Morgan had gotten off to such a bad start with each other. She wished that Brad would change his opinion of Morgan and that Morgan would get to know Brad as the good person he was.

"Good morning," Barbara chirped when Brad finally arrived. He looked surprised when he saw what she was doing and noticed her cheerful manner.

"My, aren't we chipper this morning," he said with a laugh.

"Brad, I have to tell you something." Barbara gave him her sweetest smile. "I don't know how to thank you for what you did yesterday, but if you ever do anything like that again, I'm going to break both your legs."

"Oh. I assume I scared a little starch into the man's spine?" Brad replied with a self-satisfied smile.

"Actually, you made a complete ass of yourself. But I'll let it pass. All's well that ends well."

"Am I going to be invited to a wedding?"

"Only if you promise not to molest the groom," Barbara laughed.

There was little work to be done at the Center, but Barbara hung around her office anyway, if only to try to keep her mind from dwelling constantly on Saturday. She was puttering around her office late Friday afternoon when Ron Caldwell arrived at the Center.

As he walked into her office, Barbara knew instantly that something was about to go very wrong. There was an aura of malevolence around Caldwell that she had sensed the first time they met, and she felt it again as he took the seat in front of her desk without an invitation or a word of greeting. He looked uncomfortable in his clothes, and his eyes still seemed cold and hard even when he smiled.

"Ms. Danbury, I'm Ron Caldwell. I work for Mr. Newman," he said stiffly as he looked furtively around the office.

"I remember you," she said politely. "We met at Mr. Newman's office after my dog bit you."

"Yes," Caldwell said uncomfortably, as if he didn't want to remember the incident. "I'm here representing Mr. Newman on a very important matter."

Barbara didn't reply. She looked directly at Caldwell and waited for him to continue.

"I hope you can understand the delicacy of the problem we have here," Caldwell said after clearing his throat. "Your, uh, condition isn't very good campaign fodder."

Barbara frowned. Whatever he was getting at, she had a feeling she wasn't going to like it.

"I understand you are due in April. You realize that the primary is the month before, don't you?"

"I know when the primary is," Barbara replied slowly. "I don't understand what difference it makes."

"Do you have any idea what it will do to the campaign if the candidate's wife has a baby less than nine months after the wedding—even if it is after the elections?"

"I'm sorry. I can't arrange to carry my child for eleven months if that's what you're after. Nine months is the limit."

"Mr. Newman will be made to look publicly, uh, promiscuous," Caldwell replied.

"Mr. Newman has been playing on his reputation as a 'man about town' for some time," Barbara reminded him.

"There's a great deal of difference between having the image of a swinging bachelor and fathering a child out of wedlock," Caldwell said without a trace of humor. "The voters won't stand for it. He'll lose the religious vote, the women's vote, and the senior citizens' vote, among others. It would be a disastrous blow to his election chances."

"And what do you propose I should do about it?" Barbara asked sharply. She definitely didn't like the turn that this conversation was taking.

"There are several options open," Caldwell replied without emotion. "One would be for you to visit a clinic . . ."

Barbara was slackjawed at his suggestion and couldn't even frame a reply to such a callous idea.

"We would cover your expenses, of course," Caldwell continued, misreading her reaction.

Barbara's veins were suddenly filled with ice. "Does Morgan know that you're here?" she asked in a voice that seemed to be coming from far away.

"I represent Mr. Newman's interests here, as I do in many other matters," Caldwell said smugly.

"Get out of my office," Barbara said coldly.

"If you're morally opposed to abortion, there are other alternatives," Caldwell continued.

"I'm not interested," Barbara replied. She could barely stop herself from wringing Caldwell's neck.

"You don't understand." he went on. "How can we be sure you won't publicize an embarrassing story right before the election?" Caldwell opened his briefcase and took out a checkbook. "Perhaps we could pay your way on a little vacation," he said unpleasantly. Barbara watched in amazement as he wrote out a check and slid it across her desk.

"If I knew any words to describe what you are, I would never say them," Barbara said with rising anger. "I want you out of my sight." Her voice rose in volume. "And I don't want to have to live in a city where people put up with you," she said even louder. "Take your checkbook and get out of here!" she shouted. "And you can tell Mr. Newman that there's no need to worry about my showing up with an embarrassing story at any time—in fact, he'll never hear from me again."

She picked up the check and tore it furiously into tiny shreds before throwing them at Caldwell. They fluttered impotently into the air and scattered onto her desk. Barbara desperately needed something more satisfying to throw, just to keep herself from falling apart, and when her hand settled on a paperweight, she whizzed it past Caldwell's ear. It crashed against the wall behind him, and Barbara was looking for something else to throw when Brad burst into the office.

"What's going on?" he shouted. "Are you all right, Barbara?"

"Get him out of here before I kill him," Barbara screamed, pointing to the cowering man in her office.

Brad grabbed Caldwell by the scruff of his neck and muscled him out of the room, the aide sputtering and protesting every step of the way. He stumbled across the sidewalk after Brad all but threw him through the door. "I'll sue!" he shouted back from the street. Brad made a motion as if he were going to come after him, and Caldwell hurried off down the street. Brad returned to the office to find Barbara white and shaking with rage.

"What happened?" Brad asked as he shut the door.

"He sent that weasel to pay me off," Barbara said through tightly clamped jaws.

Brad frowned. "To pay you off?"

"My choice, take a long vacation or get an abortion," Barbara elaborated.

"Are you sure it was Morgan's idea?" Brad asked uncertainly.

"*You're* defending *him?*" Barbara asked incredulously.

"Hey, don't lay that on me," Brad replied defensively, "it just doesn't seem like his style. I'd be the first to call him slippery, but I just can't see him doing anything quite this low."

Barbara gathered up the shreds of the check and started to piece them together. She gasped when she read the amount.

"Fifty thousand dollars," she said in a voice barely above a whisper. "If that isn't proof that Morgan is behind it, I don't know what is."

"How's that?" Brad asked.

"That's a lot of money. Caldwell wouldn't have con-

trol of that much. Surely Morgan would have to
approve an amount that big."

"Don't jump to conclusions," Brad said slowly.

"When did you join the Morgan Newman fan club?"
Barbara snapped.

"I haven't," Brad said softly. "But I want things to
work out for you, Barbara. I want you to be happy, and if
this is true . . ." He shrugged.

Barbara stopped and took a good look at Brad, maybe
the first really clear picture she had of him. She had
appreciated his respect, been irritated by his moods,
admired his talent, and enjoyed his company, but she
had never guessed at this enormous capacity to care
about other people. She suddenly understood why Brad
was such a difficult person. He had to be. He had to
have that gruff armor to protect the sensitive person he
truly was. Brad didn't just sympathize with her; he
shared her pain.

"Oh, Brad," she said in a voice that trembled with
emotion. "I'm going to be okay, really. In fact, I think
I'm going to feel fine as soon as I tell a certain person
just what I think of him." Tears welled up in her eyes,
making lies of her words.

Barbara picked up the phone and dialed Morgan's
office. As she waited to be put through, she tried to
think of what she was going to say, but her mind was in
as much turmoil as her churning stomach.

"Barbara, I'm glad you called." Morgan's voice was
cheerful on the other end of the line. "I wasn't going to
call you, but—"

Barbara didn't wait for him to finish his sentence.
"You didn't have to send Caldwell to get rid of me," she
said coolly.

There was a long pause at the other end of the line.
"Come again?" Morgan finally asked in a puzzled tone.

"All you had to do was say you weren't ready to get married," Barbara continued, barely controlling her voice.

"I—"

"The money was the real insult," Barbara interrupted flatly. "What would make you think you had to buy me off? I wouldn't have caused your precious campaign any trouble."

"What money?" Morgan asked in frustration. "Barbara, what are you talking about?"

"You know, Morgan, I should never have started with you in the first place. I don't know what could have made me so blind. I'm generally a better judge of character."

"What does this have to do with Ron?" Morgan asked, hoping that another approach might yield more information.

"It has nothing at all to do with Ron, now that I think about it," Barbara replied bitterly. "I really ought to call him and apologize for the way Brad treated him. It wasn't his fault. After all, he was just bringing me your message. I never realized you wouldn't have the guts to do your own dirty work."

"What message?" Morgan shouted into the phone.

"What really makes me sick is the way you're trying to pretend you don't know what I'm talking about. Aren't you even man enough to admit what you've done?" Barbara's voice began to tremble despite her best efforts to keep it steady.

"Barbara," Morgan pleaded, "give me a break. I don't have the slightest idea what you're talking about."

"Oh, no? You didn't okay the check Caldwell tried to give me? If you think that I believe he wrote a fifty thousand-dollar check out of his personal account you're out of your mind," Barbara retorted.

"Fifty thousand! For what?"

"Stop it! I'm not that naive, Morgan. I don't buy your acting ignorant."

There was a long silence as Barbara stood clutching the phone to her ear. When Morgan finally spoke, his voice was carefully controlled. "Barbara, two days ago you said you loved me. But I find that very hard to believe when you don't even trust me enough to let me find out what's going on. I'm telling you that I don't know what you're talking about, and I'm asking you, in the name of everything we've meant to each other, to tell me what happened. If my aides are sneaking around giving away money on the sly, I want to know about it."

"Ron Caldwell just left here," Barbara replied angrily. "He gave me a check for fifty thousand dollars to either have an abortion or disappear until after the general election."

There was another long silence. Then, "Barbara, how can you believe I'd send him on such an errand?" His voice was filled with pain.

"I don't want to believe it, but I can't believe anything else when I think about all that money just floating around. I can't believe that you'd run such a sloppy organization that that kind of money wouldn't be missed."

"I swear I didn't know anything about this. I can't believe it happened. Paying you off to get rid of you would be the last thing I would do. I still want to marry you. Can you give me a couple of hours to find out what's going on?"

"I wish I could believe you," Barbara cried into the phone. "But I'm sick to death of this roller coaster I've been on ever since I met you. One week everything is rosy, the next everything crashes. I thought I was getting to know you, but now I'm afraid I don't have the slightest idea who you are. The man I loved could never have done a thing like his, but I'm not sure the man I loved even exists. I'm just worn out from all these ups and downs. I'm sorry." Barbara hung up the receiver without letting Morgan reply.

She stood for several moments staring at the phone. Could Morgan be telling the truth? she wondered. Had he ever told the truth? She had no answers to her questions.

"Are you sure you're all right?" Brad asked gently.

Barbara nodded and sat down heavily in her chair.

"Let me take you home," Brad offered. "I'll bring my car around."

"No, thank you, I think I'd like to walk," Barbara said faintly. Brad looked as if he wasn't sure it was a good idea, but Barbara insisted. "I just want to be alone for a little while."

"Barbara, you may be too stubborn to accept a ride, but remember, if you need anything I'll always be around to help you."

Barbara turned away to hide the tears that were coming back to her eyes.

She walked home slowly, taking a long look at every apartment building and street corner along the way. She stopped for a moment at the spot where she had met Ossie, remembering the night her purse had been snatched. The memory brought a twinge of regret as it led to thoughts of what had come later. She lingered on the steps of her building, waiting to remember every detail. This run-down, grimy neighborhood had been her home since spring; though that wasn't a long time, Barbara knew the place would always be a part of her because of all the happy and sad things that had happened to her here.

When she finally went inside, she felt more

exhausted than she could ever remember. She opened a can of dog food for Bogey and changed his water, then went into her bedroom to lie down.

When she woke to the sound of her phone ringing, her heart jumped and she answered the call eagerly. To her disappointment, it was a wrong number.

Barbara asked herself what she had been hoping for, but she knew the answer; she had somehow hoped that it would be Morgan, with an explanation that would make everything all right again. It's a vain hope, she scolded herself. There was no possible explanation for what had happened.

The evening dragged along, and when she finally went back to bed she slept fitfully. After a light breakfast of tea and toast early the next morning, Barbara dressed in a pair of old jeans and a T-shirt and started the mournful task of packing her belongings to ship them back to New York.

She had saved most of her boxes from her first move, folded flat in the back of a closet. She opened out the cardboard crates and carefully reinforced them, then began methodically wrapping all her belongings in old newspapers. The task occupied her through the day, and she only stopped for a quick lunch at noon.

By late afternoon, Barbara was ready to start disassembling her stereo. She planned to have the entire process complete by Sunday. She could call the movers on Monday, then go back to the Center and clean out her desk while the movers emptied her apartment.

All day long, a part of her that she couldn't control was praying for the phone to ring. She chided herself over and over for the silly hope that somehow Morgan would make things right and stop her from leaving, but the part of her that dreamed of love and happiness refused to let go. Yet no matter how hard she concentrated on the phone, it hung silently on the wall, refusing to grant her wish.

Too tired to cook, Barbara called out for a pizza. When it arrived, she turned on the television, if only to break the silence while she ate her meal. The six o'clock news was beginning and she might have changed the channel or turned the set off, but she was too weary to get up and cross the room to the set.

"A surprise development in the congressional campaign came at noon today," the anchorman said as the broadcast began. "Political analysts were astounded when Morgan Newman, front-runner in the Democratic race for the House of Representatives seat now held by John Donaldson, announced that he was withdrawing from the primary and from politics in general."

Barbara's jaw dropped in surprise. A piece of pepperoni fell unnoticed into her lap, and Bogey eagerly gobbled it down.

The scene shifted to the steps of city hall, the spot where Morgan had given so many press conferences in the past. He was standing in his accustomed place, but looked nothing like the man Barbara had known. His shoulders were slumped, his eyes were dull, and he actually looked uncomfortable, as if he wished the cameras and microphones would go away and leave him in peace.

"Ladies and gentlemen," he said, holding up his hands for silence. "I'm going to read a brief statement. I will not be answering questions afterward." There was a surprised murmur from the crowd of reporters.

Morgan took a piece of paper from his jacket pocket and started to read without looking up at his audience. "In the two terms I have spent in the Chicago City Council, you, the working press, and I, the working politician, have had our ups and downs. You have often wanted more information than I have wanted to give, and I have often wanted to give less than I should have. You have criticized me when I was off the mark and have lauded me when, by some stroke of blind luck, I did the right thing. We have often been adversaries, though there are many among you whom I have called my friends.

"In the name of that friendship, whether it was deserved or not, I am now asking for your forbearance. I have decided not to run for the Congress of the United States. Further, I have decided not to seek reelection to the Chicago City Council.

"My reasons for withdrawl from politics are personal and I hope that you will respect my privacy. Thank you."

Morgan put the piece of paper back in his pocket and the picture shifted back to the studio. "That was Morgan Newman's statement at noon today," The anchorman said. "The reasons for Councilman Newman's withdrawl have been the subject of wide speculation. Reliable sources in the City Attorney's office are hinting that Monday will bring startling revelations of graft and campaign fraud in Councilman Newman's campaign organization. Meanwhile, the top aide in the Newman organization filed charges of assault against his boss this afternoon."

The picture shifted again to show a crowd of reporters surrounding Ron Caldwell as he left the courthouse. "Mr. Caldwell, what happened this morning?" a reporter shouted as Caldwell tried to elbow his way through the crowd.

"No comment," he snarled.

"Is it true that you were in charge of a large slush fund?" another reporter cried out.

Caldwell tried to push his way through without

answering, but the reporters had closed around him and had him trapped. He looked up at the camera for a moment, revealing a dark, swollen black eye.

"I'm sorry," Caldwell said when he saw that he couldn't escape without giving some kind of answer. "The matters you are asking about will soon be in litigation and my attorney advises me that I should make no statements to the press." He scowled then pushed his way out of the crowd.

Barbara set down her piece of pizza absently, trying to absorb the meaning of what she had just seen. Maybe the political analysts didn't know what was going on, but Barbara Danbury knew exactly what had happened.

She had been wrong. Oh God, she thought, as wrong as she had ever been in her life. Morgan hadn't known what Caldwell was doing. She was astonished that Caldwell would have taken such a step without authority, but that was the only explanation that stood up in the light of the news broadcast. Morgan had gone to Caldwell and asked what he had done and had actually struck him when he found out the truth.

It was almost too fantastic to believe. In the past months she had seen Morgan happy, sad, angry, and every shade of emotion in between, yet she had never dreamed that he could possibly be incited to violence.

But there was more to the story that she didn't understand. What were all the hints about criminal charges and campaign fraud? She had to talk to Morgan—not just to find out what was going on, but to say all the things that were crowding into her mind. She had to apologize for all the terrible things she had accused him of.

Barbara dialed Morgan's apartment, but got no answer. She dialed his office, but only got hold of his answering service. She sat back down on the sofa in frustration. Where could he be? The cottage didn't have a phone, so if he was there she couldn't reach him. Barbara sighed as she thought of the cottage. That was probably where he was—as far from prying reporters as he could get.

She had just made up her mind to call Brad and ask if she could borrow his car to go up to the cottage herself, when the doorbell rang. She got up and rushed to answer it, praying every step of the way that it would be Morgan.

Her prayers were answered.

He stood outside her door looking lost and hopeless. His clothes were rumpled, his face was shadowed with stubble, and his eyes were dull. He looked beaten, as if everything he had ever cared about had been taken from him.

"May I come in?" he asked quietly.

Barbara nodded and stepped back from the door. He glanced around at the stacks of boxes, at the bare walls and shelves, and sighed. The television was still on, so Barbara went over and turned it off.

"I hoped you would have seen that," Morgan said, indicating the television. "I waited till now to come, so you'd have time to hear the news first."

Barbara's throat constricted, making it difficult to speak, but she forced the words. "I'm sorry. I was so wrong about everything, Morgan. I hope that, somehow, you can forgive me."

"You weren't wrong about anything," Morgan replied in a defeated voice. He sat down on the sofa and buried his face in his hands. Barbara sat down beside him and put a comforting hand on his shoulder, her heart aching with the pain she saw in him.

"You didn't know what Caldwell was doing," she said softly. "That's why you hit him, wasn't it?"

Morgan looked up, directly into Barbara's eyes. "I hired Ron Caldwell. I knew exactly what kind of person he was. I knew the kind of tactics he was known for and I gave him free rein to do what he thought was necessary for the good of my campaign. How can I claim I didn't know what was going on?"

Barbara blinked in surprise. "But you didn't know that he came to the Center yesterday," she said uncertainly.

"If I didn't know what Ron was doing at any specific moment, it was only because I chose not to."

"I don't understand."

Morgan took a deep breath. "Ron came to me when I was running for my first term in the council. He promised me that if I hired him, he could guarantee my election, and in the long run I could plan on holding larger and more important offices. It sounded like a good deal—at the time I was running a weak third in the polls and it didn't look like I had a serious chance. I hired him and then I turned my back. I always rationalized that it didn't matter what tactics Ron was using to keep me in office because I was doing a good job. I was an honest politician and I was doing great things for the city.

"But now I have to claim every dirty trick, every shady deal, every payoff that Ron arranged. He was doing it in my name and I have to face up to the things that he did on my behalf. It doesn't matter how many good things I've done for the city."

"What does this have to do with Caldwell coming to my office?" Barbara asked. "As long as you didn't send him . . ."

"Did you notice what account that check he gave you was drawn on?" Morgan asked.

"No, I tore it up without even looking at it. I had to piece it back together just to get the amount."

"It was on the account of the Committee for the Preservation of Cultural Heritage," Morgan explained. "The only thing is, there isn't any Committee for the Preservation of Cultural Heritage. It's a slush fund, Barbara. Certain businessmen in town are in the habit of making periodic contributions to the fund, in return for small favors—zoning variances, skipped inspections, that sort of thing. Ron administered the whole thing. I never touched it. But the fact that I pretended it didn't exist doesn't clear me of being involved. Whether or not I ever saw any money, I was still taking bribes."

"I don't care about any of that," Barbara said with a frown. "I may be selfish, but the only thing I care about is the fact that you didn't send Caldwell to get rid of me."

"Don't you understand?" Morgan asked in an agonized voice. "I'm a crooked politician."

"I love you," Barbara said firmly. "I don't care what you do for a living. I wouldn't care if you were a bank robber, as long as I was sure that you loved me."

"I don't deserve you," Morgan said in a dejected voice.

"I don't believe this," Barbara replied with a frown. "Not long ago you accused me of preparing to throw myself off a burning building for dramatic effect. Now you're doing the same thing. Why don't you go home and come back when you're through feeling sorry for yourself?"

Morgan looked up at Barbara in surprise, then started to get up and leave.

"Just a minute," she said. "Before you get out of here, what's all this nonsense about giving up politics?"

"Public office is a public trust," Morgan replied. "I've

violated that trust and I don't have the right to expect people to overlook that."

"No, Morgan. What you don't have is the right to lie down and die," Barbara said forcefully. "There are people depending on you and you owe them something."

"I owe them the grace to step down," Morgan said weakly.

"What about your kid?" Barbara asked. "When he asks what his father is, do I tell him you're a crooked politician?"

Morgan looked confused. "Tell him whatever you want," he said sadly.

"Can't you see what I'm getting at?" Barbara asked desperately. "If you just slink away now, you're going to make everything that's going to be said about you true. All right, you made a mistake and it was a big one. But nobody is wiser than the man who learns from his mistakes. You really have something to offer the people now. You understand corruption. You know how it can grow in any place that's kept secret—even when the keeper has the best intentions. You can go back now and be a genuinely honest politician because you know how to avoid corruption. You owe it to all the people who trusted you in the past to prove that their trust wasn't misplaced!"

"Barbara, that all sounds very good, but you forget that, starting Monday, some really nasty facts about my organization are going to start coming out. I've violated the single most important rule of politics—never punch out the guy who knows where the bodies are buried."

"Bodies?" Barbara asked with wide eyes.

"It's a figure of speech," Morgan replied with a sad laugh. "The point is that Caldwell is going to start telling tales that will delight the media. It won't do much for my popularity."

"So what?" Barbara said. "You're worth ten Ron Caldwells any day of the week, and most of the press knows it. You once told me that sometimes the best strategy is to tell the plain truth. Well, now is one of those times. Go on television and tell everything, right down to the last detail. Admit that you were wrong and promise that there will never be another slush fund, or payoff, or dirty trick in connection with your organization. You'd be surprised how intelligent people really are when you give them a chance, Morgan. You really messed up, but it's your responsibility to prove that there can be honest politicians. You have a responsibility to your kid to make sure that he isn't the son of a crook. And you have a responsibility to your wife to make sure she can be seen in public with you without being ashamed."

"It's too late," Morgan replied. "I already announced that I'm not running."

"Unannounce it! That will drive the reporters crazy. If they want to know why you changed your mind, say that your fiancée refused to marry you unless you ran for another term in the city council."

"You refuse?"

"No, but it sounds good," Barbara said, letting a smile spread across her face.

"You're still willing to marry me—after everything that has happened?"

"I love you."

"You're all packed to leave—"

"I'll have to unpack," Barbara replied. "Though I don't know if it's worth the effort, since I'm going to be moving in with you."

"If I campaign for another term in the council, there's going to be a lot of nasty talk," Morgan said slowly. "Are you sure you want this?"

"I'm going to be beside you every step of the way," Barbara replied. "And if anyone says anything abusive, I'll be right there to deny it. It could turn out to be a very good strategy—not many people like to talk nasty to a pregnant woman."

"What about the Calvin Foundation?"

"They're going to have to get along without me for a while. They'll manage somehow."

Morgan reached out and took Barbara's hands, pulling her close to him. "And what about the turtle?" he asked with an odd expression on his face.

"What turtle?"

"Yurtle. The one who climbed too high and fell down in the mud."

"I'm not sure," Barbara replied thoughtfully. "But if he had any sense at all, when he got back down to pond level with everyone else, he found a female turtle who believed in him and lived happily ever after."

# RAPTURE ROMANCE
# BOOK CLUB
## 〜

## *Bringing You The World of*
## *Love and Romance With*
## *Three Exclusive Book Lines*

# RAPTURE ROMANCE • SIGNET REGENCY
# ROMANCE • SCARLET RIBBONS

**Subscribe to Rapture Romance
and have your choice of two
Rapture Romance Book Club Packages.**

- **PLAN A:** Four Rapture Romances plus two Signet
  Regency Romances for just $9.75!

- **PLAN B:** Four Rapture Romances, one Signet
  Regency Romance and one Scarlet
  Ribbons Romance for just $10.45!

Whichever package you choose, you save 60 cents off
the combined cover prices plus you get a FREE Rapture
Romance.

## "THAT'S A SAVINGS OF $2.55
## OFF THE COMBINED
## COVER PRICES"

We're so sure you'll love them, we'll give you 10 days to
look over the set you choose at home. Then you can
keep the set or return the books and owe nothing.

To start you off, we'll send you four books absolutely **FREE.**
Our two latest Rapture Romances plus our latest Signet Regency
and our latest Scarlet Ribbons. The total value of all four books
is $9.10, but they're yours **FREE** even if you never buy
another book.

To get your books, use the convenient coupon on the following page.

# YOUR FIRST FOUR BOOKS ARE FREE

### Mail the Coupon below

---

Please send me the Four Books described **FREE** and without obligation. Unless you hear from me after I receive them, please send me 6 New Books to review each month. I have indicated below which plan I would like to be sent. I understand that you will bill me for only 5 books as I always get a Rapture Romance Novel **FREE** plus an additional 60¢ off, making a total savings of $2.55 each month. I will be billed no shipping, handling or other charges. There is no minimum number of books I must buy, and I can cancel at any time. The first 4 FREE books are mine to keep even if I never buy another book.

Check the Plan you would like.

☐ **PLAN A:** Four Rapture Romances plus two Signet Regency Romances for just $9.75 each month.

☐ **PLAN B:** Four Rapture Romances plus one Signet Regency Romance and one Scarlet Ribbons for just $10.45 each month.

NAME _____
(please print)

ADDRESS _____ CITY _____

STATE _____ ZIP _____ SIGNATURE _____
(if under 18, parent or guardian must sign)

## RAPTURE ROMANCE

# RAPTURE ROMANCE

**Provocative and sensual,
passionate and tender—
the magic and mystery of love
in all its many guises**

## Coming next month

**DELINQUENT DESIRE by Carla Neggers.** Meeting at a summer camp for delinquent girls, it was unlikely that cool executive Casey Gray and Hollywood agent Jeff Coldwell would give themselves to each other so freely, so passionately. Both shared an unusual secret in their pasts, but by the time the secrets were revealed, it was too late—Casey had lost her cool . . . and her heart. . . .

**A SECURE ARRANGEMENT by JoAnn Robb.** Jillian Tara Kennedy wasn't prepared for aggressive, seductive Travis Tyrell, who awakened a passion within her she couldn't deny. And even though she'd sworn never to be dependent on any man, Travis' silky caresses broke down her resistance, until she was fighting not his desire, but her own. . . .

**ON WINGS OF DESIRE by Jillian Roth.** Alaskan bush pilot Erinne Parker was intrigued by mysterious biologist Jansen Lancaster. But being swept into a blazing affair with him only confused her more, and made her wonder if she was learning to love him . . . only to have him leave her. . . .

**LADY IN FLIGHT by Diana Morgan.** At his first touch, sculptor Sabrina Melendey knew her heart belonged totally to scientist Colin Forrester. But they were as far apart as art and science, and Sabrina didn't believe that love could conquer all. . . .

# RAPTURE ROMANCE

### Provocative and sensual, passionate and tender— the magic and mystery of love in all its many guises

### New Titles Available Now

(0451)

**#65** ☐ **WISH ON A STAR by Katherine Ransom.** Fighting for independence from her rich, domineering father, Vanessa Hamilton fled to Maine—and into the arms of Rory McGee. Drawn to his strong masculinity, his sensuous kisses ignited her soul. But she had only just tasted her new-found freedom—was she willing to give herself to another forceful man?
(129083—$1.95)*

**#66** ☐ **FLIGHT OF FANCY by Maggie Osborne.** A plane crash brought Samantha Adams and Luke Bannister together for a short, passionate time. But they were rivals in the air freight business, and even though Luke said he loved her and wanted to marry her, Samantha was unsure. Did Luke really want her—or was he only after Adams Air Freight?    (128702—$1.95)*

**#67** ☐ **ENCHANTED ENCORE by Rosalynn Carroll.** Vicki Owens couldn't resist Patrick Wallingford's fiery embrace years ago, and now he was back reawakening a tantalizing ecstasy. Could she believe love was forever the second time around, or was he only using her to make another woman jealous?
(128710—$1.95)*

**#68** ☐ **A PUBLIC AFFAIR by Eleanor Frost.** Barbara Danbury told herself not to trust rising political star Morgan Newman. But she was lost when he pledged his love to her in a night of passion. Then scandal shattered Morgan's ideal image and suddenly Barbara doubted everything—except her burning hunger for him. . . .    (128729—$1.95)*

*Price is $2.25 in Canada
To order, use the convenient coupon on the last page.

# RAPTURE ROMANCE

### Provocative and sensual, passionate and tender— the magic and mystery of love in all its many guises

(0451)

#57 ☐ WINTER'S PROMISE by Casey Adams. (128095—$1.95)*

#58 ☐ BELOVED STRANGER by Joan Wolf.  (128109—$1.95)*

#59 ☐ BOUNDLESS LOVE by Laurel Chandler.
(128117—$1.95)*

#60 ☐ STARFIRE by Lisa St. John.  (128125—$1.95)*

#61 ☐ STERLING DECEPTIONS by JoAnn Robb.
(128133—$1.95)*

#62 ☐ BLUE RIBBON DAWN by Melinda McKenzie.
(128141—$1.95)*

#63 ☐ RELUCTANT SURRENDER by Kathryn Kent.
(128672—$1.95)*

#64 ☐ WRANGLER'S LADY by Deborah Benét.
(128680—$1.95)*

*Price is $2.25 in Canada

_____

### Buy them at your local
### bookstore or use coupon
### on next page for ordering.

# RAPTURE ROMANCE

### *Provocative and sensual, passionate and tender— the magic and mystery of love in all its many guises*

|   |   |   |   | (0451) |
|---|---|---|---|---|
| #45 | ☐ | SEPTEMBER SONG by Lisa Moore. | (126301—$1.95)* |
| #46 | ☐ | A MOUNTAIN MAN by Megan Ashe. | (126319—$1.95)* |
| #47 | ☐ | THE KNAVE OF HEARTS by Estelle Edwards. | (126327—$1.95)* |
| #48 | ☐ | BEYOND ALL STARS by Linda McKenzie. | (126335—$1.95)* |
| #49 | ☐ | DREAMLOVER by JoAnn Robb. | (126343—$1.95)* |
| #50 | ☐ | A LOVE SO FRESH by Marilyn Davids. | (126351—$1.95)* |
| #51 | ☐ | LOVER IN THE WINGS by Francine Shore. | (127617—$1.95)* |
| #52 | ☐ | SILK AND STEEL by Kathryn Kent. | (127625—$1.95)* |
| #53 | ☐ | ELUSIVE PARADISE by Eleanor Frost. | (127633—$1.95)* |
| #54 | ☐ | RED SKY AT NIGHT by Ellie Winslow. | (127641—$1.95)* |
| #55 | ☐ | BITTERSWEET TEMPTATION by Jillian Roth. | (127668—$1.95)* |
| #56 | ☐ | SUN SPARK by Nina Coombs. | (127676—$1.95)* |

*Price is $2.25 in Canada.

---

Buy them at your local bookstore or use this convenient coupon for ordering.

**NEW AMERICAN LIBRARY**
**P.O. Box 999, Bergenfield, New Jersey 07621**
Please send me the books I have checked above. I am enclosing $_____ (please add $1.00 to this order to cover postage and handling). Send check or money order—no cash or C.O.D.'s. Prices and numbers are subject to change without notice.

Name_____

Address_____

City _____ State _____ Zip Code _____

Allow 4-6 weeks for delivery.
This offer is subject to withdrawal without notice.

# RAPTURE ROMANCE

*Provocative and sensual,
passionate and tender—
the magic and mystery of love
in all its many guises*

(0451)

#33 ☐ APACHE TEARS by Marianne Clark.      (125525—$1.95)*

#34 ☐ AGAINST ALL ODDS by Leslie Morgan. (125533—$1.95)*

#35 ☐ UNTAMED DESIRE by Kasey Adams.      (125541—$1.95)*

#36 ☐ LOVE'S GILDED MASK by Francine Shore.
                                                          (125568—$1.95)*

#37 ☐ O'HARA'S WOMAN by Katherine Ransom.
                                                          (125576—$1.95)*

#38 ☐ HEART ON TRIAL by Tricia Graves.       (125584—$1.95)*

#39 ☐ A DISTANT LIGHT by Ellie Winslow.      (126041—$1.95)*

#40 ☐ PASSIONATE ENTERPRISE by Charlotte Wisely.
                                                          (126068—$1.95)

#41 ☐ TORRENT OF LOVE by Marianna Essex. (126076—$1.95)

#42 ☐ LOVE'S JOURNEY HOME by Bree Thomas.
                                                          (126084—$1.95)

#43 ☐ AMBER DREAMS by Diana Morgan.        (126092—$1.95)

#44 ☐ WINTER FLAME by Deborah Benét.         (126106—$1.95)
      *Price is $2.25 in Canada

**Buy them at your local**

**bookstore or use coupon**

**on next page for ordering.**